Other PaleoJoe Books

Dinosaur Detective Club Chapter Books

#1 The Disappearance of Dinosaur Sue
#2 Stolen Stegosaurus
#3 Secret Sabertooth
#4 Raptors Revenge

Hidden Dinosaurs

...and more to come...

Published by Mackinac Island Press, Inc.
an imprint of Charlesbridge
85 Main Street
Watertown, MA 02472
(617) 926-0329
www.charlesbridge.com

Library of Congress Cataloging-in-Publication Data on file
PaleoJoe's Dinosaur Detective Club #5: Mysterious Mammoths

Summary: In this adventure PaleoJoe and his Dinosaur Detective Club, Shelly, and Dakota,
help PaleoJoe search for rare blue mammoth tusks in Siberia where our heroes meet up with
their old nemesis – Buzzsaw!

ISBN 978-1-934133-43-9

Fiction

Printed and bound January 2010 by Lake Book Manufacturing, Inc. in Melrose Park,
Illinois, USA
10 9 8 7 6 5 4 3

PALEOJOE'S
DINOSAUR DETECTIVE CLUB

BOOK #5

Mysterious

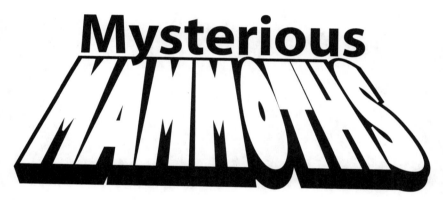

with Wendy Caszatt-Allen

Mackinac Island Press

for the love of reading

*Dedicated to the imagination
and discovery that
all children have with dinosaurs.*

MYSTERIOUS

MAMMOTHS

TABLE OF CONTENTS

TABLE OF CONTENTS

CHAPTER ONE

RUBBER BAND BOY

"Hey, Shelly! I bet you don't know this one!" The little boy jiggled and jogged up the museum steps. He was far in front of the red-haired girl who was trying to catch up to him.

"Miles, wait!" Shelly Brooks sprinted up the steps trying to catch up to the little boy. This was not easy, however, because it was Saturday and the steps were filled with visitors to the Balboa museum. The little boy in his bright orange jacket managed to dodge and bully his way between groups of people in a zigzag journey up the steps but Shelly, more polite, was forced to detour around.

He's like a renegade rubber band, thought Shelly. *He bounces here and springs back there. You never know where he will pop to next!*

Miles, his short legs carrying him in a rapid, bumping flurry though the crowd of people, was an expert distracter. Most of the people he crashed into smiled tolerantly at the small boy. Miles was five, blond, and very cute. He knew it, too. Shelly noticed the sappy look a young woman gave Miles even though he had just plowed into her with enough force to almost knock her over.

"He must be a handful," she said sympathetically to Shelly.

Shelly nodded in absolute agreement and hurried along. Still, baby-sitting Miles was usually fun and the extra money she earned doing it was great.

"Miles!" Shelly called again, hoping to get the boy to return to her.

But Miles had other ideas. "Knock! Knock!" he yelled over his shoulder. He scurried the length of one long step in a bustling hurry that forced two teenagers and a man with a newspaper to abruptly abandon that step for safer ground.

"Knock, knock, Shelly!" The little boy's shrill voice rose in the crisp air like a siren.

Everyone was looking. Shelly felt her face growing warm with embarrassment.

As far as Miles was concerned, this game of Chase was one of his favorite things to do. He knew that if he got into a crowd and pushed and bumped his way through it, it would be a challenge for Shelly to catch him.

Shelly was his second favorite baby-sitter. Dakota Jackson played Detective with him in the mall and so Miles liked him slightly better, but a good game of Chase was also a lot of fun. And besides, Miles *loved* dinosaurs, and Shelly knew more about dinosaurs than anyone—even his own mom.

"You should watch your little brother closer," a woman rubbing her foot injured by the trampling boy, scolded Shelly with a frown.

"Oh, he's not my…" Shelly started to say but was interrupted by a fresh screech from Miles.

"Shelllllllleeeeeee! KNOCK! KNOCK!"

"Who's there?" Shelly, giving up, yelled back.

"IRISH!" bellowed Miles dancing up another two steps and darting around more people.

"Irish, who?" Shelly responded in the age-old pattern of Knock-Knock jokes and plowed after him.

"Irish, you'd hurry up!" Miles yelled gleefully. "You are as slow as an *Iguanodon*!"

With a last crash into a man carrying a slim white cane, Miles bolted through the main doors of the museum and disappeared inside.

Shelly plunged forward. She narrowly avoided being beaned by the man's windmilling cane. She grabbed his arm just in time to prevent him from falling backwards down the cement steps.

"I'm very sorry," Shelly gasped.

"That is quite all right," said the man calmly. He tapped the tip of his white cane on the cement step at his feet. He wore dark glasses and Shelly suddenly realized that he was blind.

Miles should be more careful, she thought a little upset. *He could really have hurt this man.*

"I'm fine," said the man. He patted Shelly's hand with his own hand, which was knobby and wrinkled and dry as an old leaf. "The young are always in a hurry," he chuckled.

He had a very kind smile that chased waves of wrinkles around his mouth and made his bristly grey mustache dance. Shelly smiled back at him.

"Thank you for preventing me from taking a spill. Now you'd better run along and catch that small bundle of energy before he tears apart the museum!"

Red ponytail bobbing, Shelly quickly jogged up the remaining steps and entered the museum. Miles, she knew, would never dare to tear up the museum. That would make his mom supremely angry.

In fact, as Shelly anxiously scanned the crowd for Miles, she spotted his mother right away. Smiling and nodding to a group of visitors, a tall, slim woman, dressed professionally in a navy skirt and jacket, saw Shelly and waved.

Shelly waved back and looked frantically around for Miles as his mother approached.

"Hi, Shelly," the woman greeted her. She smiled in a friendly way, but Shelly was nervous. Miles's mom looked like a woman who was in charge of a great many important things—which, in fact, she was.

"Hi, Mrs. Pengelly," Shelly greeted her.

"Where's Miles?" asked Mrs. Pengelly.

Shelly's face slowly turned as red as her hair. She was finding herself in an unfamiliar situation. She did not know what to say.

Miles was the small son of Mrs. Pengelly, the Director of the Balboa Museum, and he seemed to have disappeared.

CHAPTER TWO

A WIG AND A WHISTLE

"Did you lose him?" Mrs. Pengelly asked.

"He is in the museum somewhere," Shelly was quick to reassure Mrs. Pengelly.

Mrs. Pengelly sighed. "Well, see if you can find him. I'll be in my office."

Shelly nodded, already scanning the crowd, looking for the small figure of Miles. She couldn't see him. She did, however, spot another familiar figure.

A boy wearing a tattered looking jean jacket was standing next to the Mammoth exhibit. He was busy writing something in a small notebook. And in spite of the fact that he was wearing an odd, bright green wig, Shelly recognized him at once.

It was Dakota Jackson.

Silently, Shelly tiptoed up behind him. Busy writing in his notebook, Dakota was completely unaware of her. Moving quickly Shelly whipped her hands over Dakota's eyes.

"Guess who?" she said in a low gravelly growl.

Dakota was taken completely by surprise. Stunned into frozen stillness his mind turned in high gear. Who was trying to fool him? His first thought was that it was Shelly because he expected to find her somewhere in the museum. But then he didn't think it was because he couldn't see Shelly playing this sort of joke on him. But of course that was the trouble in a nutshell—he couldn't see—and it was hard to think when you couldn't see.

"Barthelman?" He took a wild guess.

"You really are a trilobite brain," said Shelly taking her hands away.

"I knew it was you," Dakota assured her, trying not to look surprised that it was.

"No you didn't," said Shelly. "You thought I was Barthelman—Barthelman who, by the way? Not Barth Anderson I hope."

"What's wrong with Barthelman Anderson?" demanded Dakota. "He's a great football player. In fact, he's going to get me on the football team next year."

"I'm sure that's true," said Shelly, once again scanning the crowd for a glimpse of Miles, "after you do most of his math homework for him. Barthelman might be a great football player but he has the brains of a bullfrog."

Dakota made a face. Shelly, as usual, was right. Dakota had been having second thoughts about helping Barthelman and about being on the football team. Most of the boys on the team were a lot bigger than Dakota. And besides, Dakota was a fast runner. He was beginning to think he might like track better.

"In any case, I really could care less," said Shelly bringing her gaze back to Dakota's strange green wig. "And I'm almost afraid to ask, but why are you wearing a bright green wig?"

"My head was cold," Dakota frowned. In their most recent adventure Dakota had had his head shaved in order to have the nickname (or *alias* in detective language) "Butch," in honor of Butch Cassidy, the famous outlaw.

If you asked her, Shelly would quickly assure you that Dakota was known for his random acts of insanity.

"Have you heard of hats?" asked Shelly raising her eyebrows at him.

"Of course. I just didn't happen to have one handy. Are you looking for someone?" Dakota decided to change the subject.

"Miles," said Shelly.

"Oh," Dakota grinned. "Got away from you did he?"

"We were playing Chase," Shelly defended herself. "Besides, it isn't like he's never gotten away from you."

That was true. It was a recent episode of this nature that Dakota wanted badly to forget about. Miles and Dakota had been playing Detective in the busy mall while Mrs. Pengelly was having her hair done. They had been practicing the T.V. detective, Dexter North's, tactic of sussing when Miles had gotten away.

Dakota had never felt such extreme panic as he had then. He had even asked the mall security officer to help him look for the missing boy. They had eventually found Miles eating an ice cream cone on the balcony overlooking the ice rink. Mrs. Pengelly did not know about that adventure.

"Do you need help finding him?" asked Dakota.

"Please," said Shelly.

One thing, Shelly thought, *you could always count on Dakota to help even though it would most likely lead to some sort of disaster.*

"You look on that side of the museum and I'll go down this side over here."

"What should I do if I find him?" asked Dakota.

"Grab him and don't let go," said Shelly. "I'll meet you at Gamma's office."

"Got it," said Dakota.

Dakota circled around the front of the mammoth. He gave brief, critical attention to the T-Rex skeleton, but it was obvious that no small boy was hiding there. He approached the *Iguanodon* just as a cluster of visitors moved off. The *Iguanodon* stood on its mount, which was on a slightly raised platform skirted with a red felt cloth. Dakota wondered if a boy the size of Miles could squeeze under it.

Dakota stopped to look at the *Iguanodon* while he considered this possibility. Then he shook his head. *No*, he thought. That would be too tight a squeeze even for Miles.

Then, as he was about to turn away, the *Iguanodon* gave a sort of wheezy whistle and then it spoke.

"Knock, knock," it said.

CHAPTER THREE

WRESTLING GRIZZLIES

"Who's there?" asked Dakota. He recognized Miles's voice. He looked curiously at the *Iguanodon* wondering where the little boy was hiding.

"I am," said the *Iguanodon*.

"I am who?" asked Dakota getting down on his hands and knees and poking along the red felt skirting of the *Iguanodon* base. The voice was sounding a little muffled. Maybe Miles *was* under the platform somehow.

"I am really, really, really stuck," the *Iguanodon* gasped. "Help, Dakota!"

Dakota had found a small opening in the base of the platform. He stuck his hand in and found a small shoe, attached to a small leg.

Miles Pengelly.

"Hang on," said Dakota. He got down flat on his stomach, his cheek pressed against the cool linoleum, and reached both arms under the platform grabbing Miles by the legs. Squirming and wriggling on the highly polished museum floor, he at last managed to slowly pull a very dusty Miles out from under the *Iguanodon* platform.

"Thanks, Dakota," Miles grinned up at his friend and then sneezed. "Why is your hair green? It looks like frog boogers."

"No it doesn't," said Dakota wondering if frogs had such things. The two of them were sitting on the floor resting their backs against the platform of the *Iguanodon*.

"Guess what dinosaur I don't like," said Miles. And then before Dakota could answer he continued, "*Iguanodons*. They are too dusty."

Miles let loose a large and snotty sneeze to prove it. He wiped his nose on his coat sleeve, looked at Dakota and started to laugh.

"Come on, Miles," said Dakota laughing too. People were beginning to notice them. "We have to find Shelly."

Dakota helped Miles brush off most of the dirt and dust and the two of them made their way through the growing museum crowd toward the office of Gamma Brooks, Shelly's grandmother. Shelly spotted them before they reached the office.

"Hi, Shelly," said Miles. "I got stuck under the *Iguanodon.*"

Shelly grabbed his small chubby hand just to make sure he wouldn't scoot away again. "Thanks, Dakota," she said relieved to have Miles back in control. "Come on Miles. Your mom is waiting for you."

"Hey Shelly," said Miles, trotting obediently beside his baby-sitter. "What do you call a really big dinosaur that has been in a really big crash?"

"Very-saur?" asked Dakota as he followed them.

Miles snorted a laugh. "No! Guess again!"

Shelly rolled her eyes at Dakota. "I give up, Miles," she said. "Tell us."

Miles giggled. "A T-Wrecks!"

"Very funny," Shelly assured him and knocked rapidly on the door to the Museum Director's office.

"Come in!" called out Miles's mom.

Shelly pushed open the door and Miles pulled free from her hand to hurtle himself into the room. He dashed around the big glass-topped desk and catapulted into the arms of his mother who scooped him up with a loud smacking kiss on his cheek.

"Miles," she scolded, with a big sappy grin. "Did you run away from Shelly?"

"We were playing Chase," Miles explained. "I would have given up except an *Iguanodon* sat on me and I couldn't move until Dakota came and pulled me out. It was very scary."

Someone laughed. It was a deep rumbling laugh full of good humor. For the first time Shelly noticed that there was someone else in Mrs. Pengelly's office.

It was the elderly man with the slim white cane and dark glasses. As he laughed he tilted his head back and his big teeth flashed under the bristly grey mustache cuddled on his upper lip.

"Oh, what a time it is when you are very young," he said.

Mrs. Pengelly smiled and sat Miles on the corner of her desk. "Shelly and Dakota, this is Mr. Zephaniah. He is here to see PaleoJoe. I wonder if you two would be so kind as to escort him to the Tombs."

"Of course," said Shelly.

"Sure," echoed Dakota.

Both of them were very curious about why this man wanted to see PaleoJoe.

"Shelly Brooks and Dakota Jackson often help PaleoJoe with his cases," Mrs. Pengelly introduced them to her visitor.

"Is that so?" said Mr. Zephaniah. He smoothed his finger over his mustache. The dark glasses over his eyes made it difficult to read his expression. "I have a mystery for PaleoJoe. And it might be one that will require wrestling with grizzlies. Young people are often very good at that."

"Grizzlies as in grizzly bears?" asked Shelly, thinking she would rather not wrestle with anything that had sharp teeth and could eat her for breakfast.

23

"I'm speaking figuratively," said Mr. Zephaniah. "What I mean by wrestling with grizzlies, is that this particular mystery may take a certain amount of daring and courage."

Shelly grinned knowingly at Dakota.

"This way, please," said Dakota grinning back at Shelly. He politely opened the door.

Mr. Zephaniah hooked a hand under Shelly's elbow to be guided through the museum. Shelly felt a tingle of excitement. A new adventure was about to begin.

CHAPTER FOUR

THE SECRETS OF OLD STAIRS

"I'll show you how to find PaleoJoe, too," Miles yelled and catapulted himself off his mother's desk. He barged past Dakota and grabbed onto Mr. Zephaniah's other hand.

"Whoa! Slow down Grizzly Wrestler," said Dakota, quickly pulling his foot out of the way of being trampled on by Miles's sudden stampede. He got a sympathetic wave from Mrs. Pengelly. Her phone was ringing and there wasn't much she could do at the moment to retrieve her excitable son.

Dakota gave her a thumbs up and closed her door. It looked like Miles was going to be their responsibility a little bit longer. Dakota wondered if Shelly would split her day's baby-sitting money with him.

"To get to the Tombs we need to walk down some steps," said Shelly to Mr. Zephaniah.

"They are very talkative steps," said Miles bouncing along beside the elderly man and getting tangled up with the cane. "Sometimes Dakota can even get them to sing, right Dakota?"

"Or, would you rather take the elevator?" asked Shelly. She had never guided a blind person before. Mr. Zephaniah had a light but firm touch on her elbow and, in spite of Miles's jumping about, seemed to be having no difficulty following her pace as Shelly guided them through the crowds of people.

"I hardly like to miss the opportunity to hear such an interesting staircase," said Mr. Zephaniah. "Lead on Miss Brooks."

Shelly smiled. "It should be easier than wresting grizzlies," she said.

"You'd be surprised," said Mr. Zephaniah. "Grizzlies can come in many different disguises."

"Dakota, carry me like a pirate," Miles demanded, abandoning his hold on Mr. Zephaniah.

"Okay," said Dakota and reached down to scoop Miles up and sling him over his shoulder. Miles squealed with laughter.

"Arrgh!" said Dakota.

"This way," said Shelly speeding up just a bit so she and Mr. Zephaniah could be slightly ahead of the boys.

Maybe people won't know they are with us, she thought.

"May I ask you a question young Shelly Brooks?" said Mr. Zephaniah.

"Of course," said Shelly concentrating on guiding him around the exhibits.

"Do you have red hair?"

Shelly was so surprised that she almost bumped them into a large woman who had stopped suddenly to read a plaque by an exhibit of South American seashells.

"How did you know that?" she asked.

Mr. Zephaniah smiled and nodded his head. "It's a little game I like to play," he said. "I try to guess the color of a person's hair by some of their characteristics.

For example, you seem to be smart and responsible. If you have helped PaleoJoe before then you must also be brave and determined."

"Thanks," said Shelly, pleased with the compliment. She glanced over her shoulder to see if Dakota had heard, but discovered that he was so busy jiggling Miles up and down on his shoulder that he wasn't paying much attention to anything else.

"Um, what color do you think Dakota's hair is?" she asked.

"That's a tough one," said Mr. Zephaniah. He scratched his head, which, Shelly noticed, was covered with thick graying hair, cut very short, but not too short. Shelly thought it looked nice and wondered what it said about Mr. Zephaniah.

"I've been trying to puzzle it out," said Mr. Zephaniah. "I want to say his hair is some strange color like purple or green except hair doesn't grow in those colors, does it? Unless, of course, he's bald." Mr. Zephaniah laughed.

Shelly's mouth hung open in imitation of her favorite prehistoric fish, the *Dunkleosteous.* Mr. Zephaniah shrugged. "I may have to be around him a little longer to get it," he said.

"Oh no, you got it just fine," Shelly assured him and described Dakota's wig. Mr. Zephaniah chuckled. "He must be a boy of great imagination," he said.

"Great trouble really," said Shelly.

When they reached the stairwell leading to the

Tombs, Dakota put Miles down. The little boy was getting heavy and anyway Dakota knew Miles would enjoy making the stairs squeak for Mr. Zephaniah.

But first Miles had to yodel.

"Yodel-lay-eee-oooo!" Miles cupped his hands around his mouth and yodeled up the stairwell listening intently to the echoes. "That was a good one," he said.

"Come on, Miles," Shelly urged him. "There are fourteen steps here, Mr. Zephaniah," she explained. "Five, and then a landing, and then nine more."

"I understand," said Mr. Zephaniah and tapped his white cane along the floor until he discovered the first step.

Miles tumbled down the stairs ahead of everyone and Shelly could hear him bouncing and jiggling on steps seven and eight, the steps with the most squeakability. Mr. Zephaniah laughed.

"These steps sure have a lot of secrets to tell," he said as he carefully shuffled down each one guided by Shelly.

"What secrets are they telling you?" asked Dakota.

Mr. Zephaniah paused to listen to the echoing squeaks as Miles jumped from one to the next. "I think it might have to do with mysteries and treasures and ancient times," he said. "But I'm not really sure. I don't speak ancient Stair. Do you?"

Dakota grinned and shook his head. He didn't know how to speak ancient Stair but he did know a little bit about mysteries and treasures.

And he was hoping that Mr. Zephaniah was about to tell them a little bit more on the subject.

CHAPTER FIVE

THE GUARDIAN OF THE TOMBS

They squeaked and creaked the rest of the way down the old wooden staircase. Miles had to run back to the top twice before they could persuade him to let the stairs rest for a bit. When they reached the closed door to the Tombs, Dakota stepped forward to knock but Miles tugged at his arm.

"Let me do the knock," Miles begged.

"Of course," said Dakota. "You are the Knock-Knock expert after all."

Miles nodded seriously. He raised his small knobby fist to the large door, paused to make sure he remembered the correct knock, and then rapped out the secret code: *rap-a tat-a tattat-rap-rap!*

There was a brief silence and then, slowly, the door opened just a crack and a handsome, tailless, brown striped cat slipped out to wind around the ankles of Miles and Dakota.

"Saber!" Miles happily reached out to pet the bobtailed cat that was now purring almost as loudly as Miles had yodeled.

"Hi, Saber," said Shelly also stroking the soft cat in greeting. Saber gave a happy little *purp* sound—an interesting cross between a purr and a happiness burp —and sat down on Dakota's foot just as the head of a woman peered around the edge of the door.

"Who dares to enter the Tombs?" said the woman in a loud and deep voice. And then in a sort of hoarse whisper she said, "Is that good?"

Shelly nodded, a quick smile chasing across her face. "It's good," she said, "only don't ask because it ruins it."

"Oh, right," said the woman. "I'll try again."

The door slammed closed.

Dakota looked at Shelly. Shelly shrugged. "Mike is still pretty new at this," she explained to Mr. Zephaniah, but she didn't go into the details of their last adventure and the reason why Mike was the new chief of maintenance at the Balboa. It was still hard to believe the damage the criminal known as Buzzsaw had managed to cause in their most recent encounter.

"Better give her another chance, Miles," said Dakota.

"Okay," said Miles and rapped out the code again: *rap-a tat-a tattat-rap-rap!*

The door slowly creaked opened. The woman peered around the edge. "Who dares to enter the Tombs?" asked Mike in a loud deep voice.

"We do!" sang out Miles, Shelly, and Dakota together.

Mr. Zephaniah cleared his throat. "As well as I, too," he said politely with a slight bow.

"To gain entrance to the Tombs you must prove yourself worthy by answering the Explorer's Question!" boomed the woman making her face furrow into a terrible frown.

With her red hair, only just a little streaked with gray, and her oversized blue, workman's overalls, Shelly thought that, actually, Mike fit the role of Guardian to the Tombs pretty well.

"We're ready," Shelly assured her.

"Who wants to go first?" asked Mike.

"I do! I do!" shouted Miles waving his skinny arm in the air and flapping his hand like a small flag.

"Okay, then," said Mike in a very solemn tone. "Prepare yourself, young explorer!"

"I'm ready," said Miles. His eyes were wide and eager. Shelly had to hide a smile. She wondered if she and Dakota looked like that when they presented themselves for the Explorer's Question.

"What did the *Dryosaurus* say to his friend when they were sneaking past the hungry *Allosaurus*?" Mike narrowed her eyes at Miles in an evil squint.

"Do you think he-saurus?" Miles shouted.

"You have answered correctly! Enter Brave Explorer and search out the Unknown!"

With a whoop, Miles was through the door and because his shoe had come untied and his shoelace was waving about in a very interesting fashion, Saber decided to chase after him. Shelly could hear the commotion of the chase as the small cat and the small boy raced away along the long corridor that led to PaleoJoe's office.

"Thanks, Mike," said Shelly smiling. "That was really nice of you to have a question special for Miles."

She walked forward guiding Mr. Zephaniah expecting to be allowed to follow Miles. She was surprised when Mike blocked her way.

"Not so fast Young Explorer," said Mike in her deep voice. "Only those brave enough to answer a question may enter. You did not answer a question. You cannot enter!"

CHAPTER SIX

SHELLY'S QUESTION

"It's usually just one question for the group though," said Shelly trying to peer past Mike to see where Miles had gone. The last thing she needed was for the little boy to disappear again.

"Old Rules," said Mike. "Now I'm here and there are New Rules. *Each* Explorer must answer a question. There will no longer be anyone getting through on the brains of someone else. You must answer your own question!"

"But Mike," Shelly argued. "This is Mr. Zephaniah and he has an important mystery for PaleoJoe."

"All the more reason he should pass the Explorer's Question first," snapped Mike, glaring at Mr. Zephaniah.

"Does that woman have red hair, too?" whispered Mr. Zephaniah to Shelly.

"Yes," Shelly hissed back.

"Then I suggest we do as she says," Mr. Zephaniah whispered.

"Okay," said Shelly giving in. "Dakota, you go next."

"Right," said Dakota. He knew Mike would ask him something challenging. He squared his shoulders and stepped forward.

"Prepare yourself!" said Mike. Then she got a good look at the wig Dakota was wearing.

"Why are you wearing a green wig?" she asked him.

"Because," said Dakota with great dignity, "my head was cold."

And he marched past Mike before she could stop him.

"Hey wait!" said Mike grabbing for the back of Dakota's shirt collar. She missed and Dakota didn't stop. "That wasn't the question."

"Too late," said Dakota over his shoulder. "You asked. I answered. Them's the Rules."

"Hey!" yelled Shelly at Dakota's rapidly retreating back. "That wasn't fair!"

"You're just mad because you have to answer your own question," Dakota called back.

"It wasn't even correct grammar," said Shelly indignantly as Dakota marched out of sight.

Mike glared at Mr. Zephaniah and Shelly. The look in her eye made Shelly swallow nervously. "Who's next?" Mike demanded.

"You go, Mr. Zephaniah," said Shelly. She did not want to be next after that trick. *Dakota,* she thought in disgust. *Why was he always causing trouble?*

"Very well," said Mr. Zephaniah calmly. "You may ask your question, Guardian."

A small smile tugged the corner of Mike's mouth. "How do you remove a hard-water stain from a sink?"

Shelly's mouth popped open in protest. What kind of question was that? But before she could say anything Mike put a warning finger to her lips. Shelly got the message. For some reason Mike thought that this was a good question for their guest.

And knowing Mike and her fascination for cleaning stuff, thought Shelly, *she probably really wants to know.*

"Hmmm…" Mr. Zephaniah ran a knobby finger through his short mustache. "There are many kinds of commercial products designed for such things."

"Tried them," said Mike. "This is a very stubborn stain."

"Well, I've heard that a package of dry lemonade drink mixed with some very hot water does the trick," said Mr. Zephaniah. "It's the lemon you know. An old secret my own mother used."

Mike smiled. "You have answered correctly—I hope—you have no idea how crazy that stained sink is driving me!"

Shelly hid a smile behind her hand. Mike the Clean Freak—if they weren't careful, they would soon find themselves wielding a broom, or mop, or dust cloth.

"Enter Brave Explorer," said Mike to Mr. Zephaniah.

"I guess I'll have to wait for Shelly," said Mr. Zephaniah. "She's my guide."

"Right then, Miss Torch," said Mike using a nickname she had given Shelly in their last adventure when Shelly had first met Mike. "I'm sure you are expecting a question about paleontology."

Shelly nodded.

"I won't disappoint you then," said Mike. She folded her arms and raised an eyebrow at Shelly. "Who is credited with finding the world's first ichthyosaur?"

"Oh dear," said Mr. Zephaniah. "That sounds like a very difficult question."

"It is a difficult question," said Mike in a tone of satisfaction. "But only the bravest of explorers are expected to face such questions. The questions have to be hard."

Out of the corner of her eye, Shelly saw Mr. Zephaniah tighten his mouth as though he expected that she would be unable to answer the question. Mike leaned in the doorway and frowned a mighty frown as she tried to look pirate-fierce.

"Well, Miss Torch," said Mike. "What is your answer?"

Shelly smiled a secret smile behind her hand as she pretended to think.

Oh no, Mike, Shelly thought. *You're not going to get my answer that easily.*

Shelly had that look in her eye that spelled danger. Had Dakota been there he could have warned Mike. But he wasn't and so Mike had no clue what she was in for.

CHAPTER SEVEN

A PREHISTORIC DUCK

"Well," said Shelly. "Ichthyosaurs lived in the seas of the Mesozoic period."

Mike nodded. "Common knowledge. Go on."

"They were similar to dolphins except that they had a long, pointed snout full of sharp teeth. They had fins for steering and a powerful tail that was shaped like a crescent."

"Well that is very intelligent, young Shelly Brooks," applauded Mr. Zephaniah. "It sounds to me as though you know all about those ichthyosaur fellows. What do you think, Ms. Guardian?"

"I think she hasn't answered the question yet," said Mike suspiciously.

Shelly scratched her head. "Well, I guess that's right," she said.

"And I guess that means that you don't know the answer," said Mike a bit surprised. She never thought it would be that easy to stump Shelly.

Shelly smiled because of course she wasn't stumped at all. "I guess you would be wrong," said Shelly with a smirk. "The person who is said to have found the first ichthyosaur is Mary Anning. She was 12 years old and she excavated it herself!"

"Brilliant!" exclaimed Mr. Zephaniah and tapped his cane on the polished floor in applause.

"Come along, Mr. Zephaniah," said Shelly tucking the elderly man's arm under her elbow. "This way into the Tombs!"

Mike stood aside and let them pass. She gave Shelly's ponytail an affectionate tug as the girl bounced by.

Shelly and Mr. Zephaniah reached the old oak door to PaleoJoe's office just as a thunderous crash sounded from inside.

"MILES!" It might have sounded like the roar of a T-Rex but Shelly recognized it as PaleoJoe.

Suddenly, the door flew open and Miles scooted out narrowly missing Shelly and Mr. Zephaniah. This was a good thing because Miles seemed to have transformed himself into something yellow and fuzzy. He was laughing and screeching and flapping his skinny arms up and down.

"Look Shelly!" he cackled dancing in a circle around her. "I'm a prehistoric duck!"

"You're a prehistoric mess!" scolded Mike, suddenly appearing beside Shelly. Mike whipped out a pair of blue rubber gloves and snapped them on her hands. Then the Guardian of the Tombs moved with lighting quick speed and captured the squawking, flapping Miles. Holding him at arms length to avoid the gooey yellow stuff, which covered Miles she said, "You're coming with me, young sir. It's bath time!"

Miles let out one last ear-piercing shriek and then Mike bundled him off. A strange calm rippled through the Tombs.

"I guess we better see what happened," said Shelly. Mr. Zephaniah nodded and squeezed her elbow in encouragement. Together they cautiously pushed open the door and stepped into PaleoJoe's office.

"Oh no!" said Shelly as she took in the scene of disaster that confronted her.

Dakota, his green wig crooked, was down on his hands and knees with a fistful of rag. He was trying to mop up a widening puddle of yellow paint, but as hard as he was trying, the paint refused to do anything but

43

smear. Nearby a large box lay on its side, its contents of bones spilling out onto the floor along with a small truckload of fuzzy, fiber-like packing material.

And on the floor, in the very center of the puddle of smeary yellow paint, sat PaleoJoe wearing wisps of packing material in his beard and hair. He looked like a scarecrow off his pole. His eyes were squeezed tightly closed. His face was very red and he appeared to be counting.

"He tried to duck when Miles knocked over the box of bones," explained Dakota.

"Another prehistoric duck," observed Mr. Zephaniah. "Have I come at a bad time?"

CHAPTER EIGHT

A MAN OF ACTION

PaleoJoe's eyes snapped open. "Malachi Zephaniah! Is that really you?"

"It's really me," Mr. Zephaniah chuckled. "The question is, is that really you or have we been invaded by yellow, packing material monsters from the basement of the Balboa?"

PaleoJoe scowled. "I was wrestling grizzlies, Malachi," he said. "A practice I believe you know something about."

Mr. Zephaniah laughed and nodded his head. "I would be surprised to find you doing anything else, PaleoJoe," he said.

"Come in, Malachi," said PaleoJoe, carefully extracting himself from the middle of the paint puddle.

"Shelly, can you find Mr. Zephaniah a seat somewhere safe until we get this mess cleaned up?"

"Where is safe?" grumbled Dakota swiping, at the oozing yellow puddle. "With Miles on the loose none of us are safe."

"Take him into my office," said Mike appearing in the doorway with a bucket and mop. "I've sent Sir Miles back to his mother and locked the Tombs."

"That's the best news I've heard all day," whispered Shelly to Mr. Zephaniah as she led him around the corner to Mike's office.

Mike's office was really the custodian's den. It was filled with buckets and brooms and bottles of cleaning fluid, rags, and wrenches and tools, and all sorts of equipment for keeping the Balboa spotlessly clean and running smoothly. But there was also a very comfortable brown leather couch that Shelly helped Mr. Zephaniah to sit on. Shelly perched herself on the edge of Mike's clean and orderly desk.

Through the wall they could hear sounds of PaleoJoe grumbling and the clank of the bucket and mop. In a few minutes Dakota came to join them.

"Whew," he said and collapsed onto the couch next to Mr. Zephaniah. He had a smear of yellow paint on his face and his green wig was hanging crooked over his left ear. "I think Mrs. Pengelly should give us hazard pay when we baby-sit Miles."

In a few more minutes PaleoJoe joined them. He had changed his clothes, all traces of yellow paint and packing fibers were gone, and he was carrying two steaming cups of coffee. He handed one to Mr. Zephaniah. And then from his back pockets he pulled two frosty bottles of root beer, which he handed to Dakota and Shelly.

"It's not hazard pay," said Dakota, a big smile on his face as he popped the top of the bottle, "but I'll take it!"

"Me — *hic* — too!" said Shelly, taking too large a gulp of her fizzy drink and paying for it with instantaneous hiccups.

"It's good to see you, Malachi," said PaleoJoe seating himself on Mike's desk chair. "It's been awhile."

"Almost three years," said Mr. Zephaniah cradling his steamy cup of coffee between his gnarled hands. "It was just after that business of trilobites those villains were attempting to smuggle out of Morocco. Do you remember?"

PaleoJoe nodded his head. He was dressed in his green pants and khaki shirt as usual. *He must have a whole wardrobe of those clothes,* thought Shelly trying to hold her breath to get rid of her hiccups. She held her breath for a count of 20 and watched her friend PaleoJoe as he smoothed a hand through his short, carefully trimmed, graying beard. *And he looks like an adventurer,* she thought cautiously taking a breath to see if her hiccups had been defeated. When it appeared she had been successful she took a happy sip of her cold pop listening closely to the conversation.

"I remember we caught those ruffians right in the middle of the night as they were loading crates with the fakes," said PaleoJoe. "I also remember how you used your cane to trip the guy that intended to use my head as a punching bag."

"It was the least I could do, sir," said Mr. Zephaniah with a wide grin.

"Wow," said Dakota. "It sounds like a lot of danger. Are you some kind of undercover secret agent?"

"Yes, in a way," said Mr. Zephaniah.

"Malachi is a specialist who fights fossil related crimes," said PaleoJoe. "He taught me most of what I know. He is a man of action and a great thinker."

Dakota looked in admiration at Mr. Zephaniah. Even though he had the dark glasses, an elderly blind man with a cane did not fit the description of a man of action in Dakota's mind. Dexter North, a well known T.V. detective, with his sussing techniques, his dark reflective sunglasses, and his deadly fighting moves fit Dakota's idea of man of action.

"Amazing," he said.

"I would just bet you are asking yourself how a man that is blind can be an investigator; is that true?" asked Mr. Zephaniah.

Dakota had not wanted to sound rude but he had been wondering.

"It's a perfectly easy explanation, young man," said Mr. Zephaniah. "Most people think that you need to see to understand the complexities of the world around us. Well, it's quite true. And even though I am blind, I see too. But I don't see in the same way that you or PaleoJoe or Miss Shelly see. I see with my mind. I see with touch. I see with my ears. And I see with my nose. Do you understand?"

"Yes," said Dakota nodding his head. And he wasn't lying either. He did understand. Because Mr. Zephaniah couldn't see with his eyes, he used his other senses to figure things out.

"Then I think. And, as I'm sure you already know, a good detective must be able to think extremely well."

"I get that," said Dakota enthusiastically. Looking carefully and then thinking about what he saw was a method he sometimes employed himself. Unlike Shelly who seemed to know things immediately, Dakota sometimes needed time to sort things through.

"I don't see how you can get it," said Shelly. "There is thinking involved."

Dakota scowled at the smug look Shelly gave him. "A little radiation, too, from my powerful mind," he told her. "Better stand back."

"So what is this mystery of yours, Malachi?" asked PaleoJoe, interrupting the feud that threatened to break out between Shelly and Dakota. *Couldn't those two get along for just five minutes?* PaleoJoe thought.

"I wonder," said Mr. Zephaniah, "if any of you have heard of the legendary fossils known as the Blue Tusks?"

Dakota wasn't surprised that he hadn't, but he was surprised to see Shelly shake her head. There was something she didn't know about fossils?

Unbelievable.

"Oh yes," said PaleoJoe with a thoughtful look in his eyes. "I have heard of them. Rumors only, of course, because the Blue Tusks are indeed great and mysterious fossils that have never been found. Some people even doubt that they actually exist."

"Oh, they exist all right," said Mr. Zephaniah. "And I think I know how to find them."

CHAPTER NINE

Legend of the Blue Tusks

"What are the legendary Blue Tusks?" asked Shelly in the same breath that PaleoJoe exclaimed, "How?"

Mr. Zephaniah held up a hand. "Patience," he smiled in Dakota's direction. He had heard the rustle of paper as Dakota fished out his notebook. "A good investigator must get his facts in an orderly manner."

"I'm ready," said Dakota, pencil poised.

"Then I will begin at the very beginning, which is where all good stories start," said Mr. Zephaniah. "There is in existence a substance known as odontolite. Spell it the way it sounds, young man."

Frowning in concentration, Dakota sounded out the word.

Shelly shook her head. "Never heard of it."

"It has many other names as well," explained Mr. Zephaniah. "Some people call it ivory turquoise, fossil turquoise, or fossil toothstone. Of course it isn't turquoise at all, but it looks like it. Odontolite is created when fossil ivory is buried alongside certain iron phosphate minerals."

"Where does fossil ivory come from?" interrupted Dakota.

"Everyone knows that," said Shelly in her superior know-it-all tone that drove Dakota crazy. "Several prehistoric animals had ivory tusks but mainly the mammoth and mastodon had the largest."

"That is correct," said Mr. Zephaniah, admiration clear in his tone.

Dakota scowled and, with a very great effort, refrained from drowning Shelly in the last of his fizzy root beer. He drank it down instead hiding his annoyance with a large belch.

"Barking dust mites," he said as Shelly gave him her Shelly Look of Disapproval. He wiped his mouth with the back of his hand.

"Continue, Malachi," said PaleoJoe raising one eyebrow in warning at both Shelly and Dakota.

"Over time, the minerals leach into the tusks like a sponge absorbing water," said Mr. Zephaniah. "The minerals color the ivory a deep blue that resembles turquoise. A very long time ago, the Cistercian monks were famous for carving medieval art objects from odontolite."

53

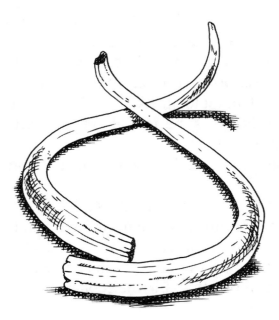

"Are the Blue Tusks art objects?" asked Dakota.

"No, although at one time, they were headed for that fate," Mr. Zephaniah paused to take a sip of his hot coffee. "The Blue Tusks are supposed to be complete, 12-foot long, unbroken mammoth tusks that have been turned to odontolite."

"I get it now," said Shelly.

Dakota wasn't sure that he did, but he carefully wrote down all the information in his Detective Notebook and pretended.

"The tusks were found," continued Mr. Zephaniah, "so the story goes, by a lay brother of the Cistercian monks. For some reason this monk hid the tusks in a place that has kept them secret for hundreds of years."

"So secret in fact that most people don't think they exist at all," said PaleoJoe. "The Blue Tusks are stories that some paleontologists tell for entertainment. Malachi, there is no evidence that they actually exist."

"Until now," said Mr. Zephaniah mysteriously.

"Go ahead then," said PaleoJoe a slight smile on his face. He was sure the Blue Tusks were just fancy, but Malachi Zephaniah had been his friend for a very long time and so PaleoJoe thought it wouldn't hurt to hear him out. "Tell us."

"Last week I received a letter from a friend of mine. He said that he had found proof of not only the existence of the Blue Tusks, but also strong evidence that pointed to where they might be found."

"What kind of evidence?" asked Dakota.

"A journal written in 1792 by the very Cistercian lay brother who claims to have found the Blue Tusks in the first place," said Mr. Zephaniah.

"Is the journal authentic?" asked PaleoJoe, interested in spite of his doubt that the Blue Tusks were real.

"I don't know," Mr. Zephaniah shook his head. "But that's why I need your help, PaleoJoe. I thought that maybe you would go with me to talk to my friend and examine the journal to see what you think. If it is authentic then someone needs to go looking for a legend."

55

PaleoJoe smiled. "I guess I would be the man to do that!"

"And I'd be the girl," said Shelly.

"I'd be the boy," said Dakota.

Mr. Zephaniah laughed, and then he became serious. "There are some dangerous stirrings in the world of fossil smuggling just now PaleoJoe. I'm concerned about the rise of a new gang of criminals. But right now I am taking a few days vacation. That should give us enough time to look at this journal and decide if it is authentic or not."

"Absolutely," said PaleoJoe. "Things are a little slow at the museum just now. Who is your friend and where can we find him?"

"Well, you know him too, of course. It's Doug Chisholm," said Mr. Zephaniah.

PaleoJoe smiled and stroked his beard. "I know Doug," he said. "Doug Chisholm is a senior research assistant at Mammoth Site. Shelly, you're going to love this!"

Shelly had already jumped up and was bouncing on her toes in a barely held in check exuberance. "Are we going to go talk to him, PaleoJoe?" she asked.

"I think we better," said PaleoJoe. Then he turned and winked at a surprised Dakota. "You'll like this too, Dakota. Mammoth Site is in South *Dakota*."

"Awesomeness!" shouted Dakota, bouncing to his feet and punching the air with his fist. Dakota had a special fondness for the two states after which he was named.

Mr. Zephaniah began to laugh as he, too, was suddenly filled with the urge for some happy bouncing.

CHAPTER TEN

A SHORT CUT TO A DEATH TRAP

"We're lost," grumbled PaleoJoe. He glared suspiciously out the car window as they passed a familiar looking gas station. "Didn't we pass that gas station 10 minutes ago?"

"No, we didn't and no, we aren't," said Shelly adjusting a setting on PaleoJoe's new GPS device. "We take another left just ahead at that intersection. Move over, PaleoJoe—you're in the wrong lane!"

"*Iguanodon* tonsils!" exclaimed PaleoJoe as he sped up.

He maneuvered the car ahead of a monster semi, all chrome and humming tires, and pulled over in front of it to be in the correct lane for his turn.

"Now, just ahead another six miles and then we make a right," said Shelly.

"Some shortcut," muttered PaleoJoe, glancing in his rear view mirror and seeing only truck grill from the monster semi.

Shelly squirmed in her seat but didn't say anything. It had been her idea to break in PaleoJoe's new GPS device on this trip. She thought an adventurer, like PaleoJoe, ought to know how to use the latest in technology.

Unfortunately, PaleoJoe preferred old-fashioned maps. In fact, he had even been known to actually stop and talk to people to get directions.

They were trying to get to the Mammoth Site center. Shelly, messing with the GPS device, had said she had discovered a shortcut. It was turning out to be not a very good one. It wasn't that they were lost; it was just that the route they were following wasn't short.

Still, thought Shelly in defense, *we are getting to see some interesting landscape.*

Not that it mattered much really, because no one was paying attention to it. Dakota, a little thread of drool wandering from his open mouth, was snoring in the backseat. PaleoJoe was too distracted driving though the heavy traffic. And Mr. Zephaniah…well, Shelly wasn't altogether sure how a blind person did enjoy scenery from a car.

"What time is Doug expecting us, Malachi?" asked PaleoJoe.

Mr. Zephaniah had made arrangements with

Doug Chisholm, senior research assistant of Mammoth Site, to meet with them after the visitor center closed for the evening.

Shelly was very excited. They were going to get a private tour of the indoor excavation site.

"About 6:00," said Mr. Zephaniah, checking his wristwatch.

Mr. Zephaniah had a great watch; one that Dakota, when he was awake, truly admired. It was a Braille watch, so instead of numbers it had tiny raised bumps. Mr. Zephaniah could flip the top open and run the tips of his fingers gently over the bumps to see what time it was.

"We have lots of time," he assured PaleoJoe.

And as it turned out he was right. A half an hour later PaleoJoe pulled into the parking lot of the Mammoth Site Visitor Center. They were 15 minutes early. As they walked into the Center Dakota was yawning and Shelly was intensely interested in everything around her. They were the only people going in. Everyone else was coming out because the Center was about to close.

"Thank you for visiting Mammoth Site," a cheerful woman's voice rippled over an intercom system addressing the visitors. "The Visitor's Center will be closing in 10 minutes. Please come and see us again."

PaleoJoe led them to the front desk. Mr. Zephaniah explained to the lady of the intercom announcement who they were and what they wanted.

"Oh yes," she said. "Mr. Chisholm is expecting you." With a bright smile she directed them to the indoor excavation site.

The excavation site was a huge pit of shelved and cut caramel colored stone on which the partially excavated skeletal remains of ancient animals lay exposed. Encircled by a railed wooden walkway, an observer could see into the pit and get good views of the work being done in this wonderful, cliff-like place.

"Look, PaleoJoe!" exclaimed Shelly, her eyes wide as she leaned over the wood railing of the walkway, peering down into the excavation site. "Those are mammoth skulls. Look at those tusks!"

A balding man wearing a blue shirt, who had been kneeling near some of the giant bones in the pit, stood up and looked at Shelly.

"Malachi? PaleoJoe? Is that you? Greetings! Come on down and bring those bright looking, inquisitive young people with you," the man called, waving a welcome.

"I'll stay here, PaleoJoe," said Malachi. "Go ahead and take Shelly and Dakota down there."

"Come on, Dakota," said Shelly impatiently marching off. "Let's go."

"It's this way, Shelly," PaleoJoe nodded his head in the opposite direction. "Kind of lost without a GPS device aren't you?" he teased as Shelly about-faced and marched past him.

Shelly stuck her tongue out at him. Dakota

61

laughed. Usually, he was the one getting the rude faces made by Shelly. *It makes a nice change*, he thought as he followed Shelly and PaleoJoe through a doorway, down some stairs, and out into the bumpy, shelf-like landscape of the pit.

"Welcome," said Doug Chisholm as they joined him. He cheerfully shook PaleoJoe's hand, a broad grin on his face.

"Welcome to the death trap!"

CHAPTER ELEVEN

FOSSIL TREASURE

"I'm not sure I feel happy about being welcomed into a death trap," Dakota whispered to Shelly as they carefully threaded their way between the mounds of coffee color stone and fossil.

Shelly gave him a small punch in the ribs. "It's not a death trap anymore, genius," she hissed at him. "It's a treasure house of fossils. Just look at them all!"

Dakota was looking. You had to, really, or you would plow into any of a number of fossil bones half carved out of the surfaces of the pit. Dakota carefully threaded his way around a bone, that was easily as long as he was tall, and squeezed past the spear point of a tusk that lanced through the air just about eye level.

"This is a dangerous place all right," he muttered,

feeling the pointy end of the tusk. "Could put your own eye out if you're not careful."

But no one was paying any attention to him. As usual.

"It's good to see you again, Doug," said PaleoJoe enthusiastically. "This is my young assistant, Shelly Brooks."

"Hi," said Shelly, stopping a little too suddenly so that Dakota managed to bump into her. "And this is Dakota Jackson, masquerading as the World's Biggest Klutz," she said giving him a little push back.

Dakota's heel caught on the edge of a bone. He threw out his arms for balance, whacked PaleoJoe in the stomach but managed to not fall down.

"*Oof,*" grunted PaleoJoe.

"If he becomes too annoying," said Shelly, "I'm sure we could find another sinkhole for him to visit."

Doug Chisholm chuckled. He was a stocky man, bald except for a fringe of closely cut gray hair that wrapped around the back of his head. He wore glasses, had a loud, friendly laugh, and his eyes sparkled with enthusiasm as he watched Shelly's obvious interest in the excavation site grow.

"Pleasure to meet you both," he said vigorously shaking hands with Shelly and then Dakota. "As you can see at one time this wasn't a very safe place, but I think most of the danger is in the past now." He grinned and winked at Dakota.

Dakota smiled back uncertainly. *Most* of the

danger was gone? What did that mean?

"I assume you are calling this sinkhole a death trap because it trapped all these animals somehow," said Shelly looking admiringly at the bones scattered all about her. They lay exposed like the lumpy remains of giants protruding from the rock.

"That's right," said Mr. Chisholm. "It's a fascinating story. What you are looking at is the remains of one of the deadliest enticements nature ever invented."

"What's an enticement?" asked Dakota.

"It's wanting to stuff you into your own private sinkhole," said Shelly grumpily. Why did Dakota always have to interrupt with stupid questions?

"Quiet now, Shelly," said PaleoJoe.

"Well, he asks such dumb questions sometimes," grumbled Shelly.

Dakota felt his face growing warm. He always managed to make himself look foolish in front of Shelly, he thought. He had rules. Why didn't he follow them? Rule #3 clearly stated: *Don't ask questions around annoying know-it-all girls*. And rule #4, just as important: *Never forget rule #3!*

"Never mind," said Mr. Chisholm gripping Dakota's shoulder in a friendly gesture. "There are no such things as dumb questions if a person is truly seeking knowledge. All great scientists have to ask questions. A lot of questions. And besides," Mr. Chisholm lowered his voice and whispered loudly in Dakota's ear, "If a girl insults you it just means that she likes you."

If Dakota's face had felt warm before, now it felt on fire. He figured that the blush of embarrassment that now erupted over his face, spreading from neck to forehead, could probably provide enough light to read in a very dark place.

"She doesn't like me," Dakota mumbled, but Mr. Chisholm just smiled and punched him on the arm.

I wish I had that sinkhole right about now, Dakota silently groaned. His face was so hot with embarrassment he thought he could probably light a match off his left ear. It didn't help at all that Shelly had obviously heard what Mr. Chisholm whispered. Her face was also bright red. The scowl she was working around her mouth was looking pretty scary, too.

All this and I still don't know what enticement means, thought Dakota, carefully moving away from Shelly to stand on the other side of PaleoJoe.

Leaning on the wooden railing above their heads, Mr. Zephaniah listened to the murmur of their voices as he became lost in deep thought. Around him, with the departure of the last tour group, the visitor's center had quieted down which made it easy for him to do his thinking. Several banks of the main lights were turned off leaving most of the area around him in soft shadow. The voices of employees calling back and forth, laughing together as they shut things down, drifted to Mr. Zephaniah's sensitive ears.

"Leave the pit lights on, George!" He heard

someone call. "Mr. Chisholm is still in there with visitors!"

Mr. Zephaniah's thoughts swirled around his current challenge. That rise in the criminal activity of the fossil black market had him deeply concerned. It seemed apparent that a new organized group of criminals were on the rise. They were creating quite a dangerous stir in the world of the fossil black market.

He wanted to have a chance to discuss it with PaleoJoe because one name had sifted to the surface of his investigations:

Theodore Edward Kaskia III.

That man had been PaleoJoe's graduate assistant at one time, but now it appeared that he had found something else to interest him: black market fossils.

One thing was clear to Mr. Zephaniah. If the journal proved to be authentic then PaleoJoe would have to find the Blue Tusks on his own. Mr. Zephaniah, heavily engaged with this new investigation, would not be able to go.

Still, reflected Mr. Zephaniah, *PaleoJoe has Shelly and Dakota. They will be most valuable in their assistance. And if Doug Chisholm has the evidence, then one of the greatest adventures in paleontology is about to begin.*

Mr. Zephaniah leaned on the rail and thought about the Blue Tusks. A slight rustling noise from the pit just under his rail caught his attention.

Probably just one of the employees leaving the

pit for the evening, thought Mr. Zephaniah.

An employee that really needs to take a bath, he added silently as his keen sense of smell detected the faint whiff of old tennis shoe odor.

CHAPTER TWELVE

Seeking Treasure

"Do all these skulls belong to woolly mammoths?" asked Shelly, running her fingers lightly over the bone Mr. Chisholm had been working on.

"That's a good question," said Doug Chisholm. He took a small brush from his hip pocket and gently swabbed at the bone.

Dakota scowled. *Of course,* Shelly would ask *good* questions.

"Take a look," said PaleoJoe handing Shelly his loupe. Shelly bent to examine the bone through the tiny, but powerful, magnifier.

"The answer to your question is no," said Mr. Chisholm. "We have found only three woollys here. Most of these bones belong to the Columbian mammoth.

Of course many of the bones here also belong to other
Ice Age animals like the camel and the giant short-
faced bear." Mr. Chisholm pointed out some of the
other bones nearby.

"How did all these animals get here?" asked
Dakota, risking a question. Out of the corner of his eye
he saw Shelly scowl, but she didn't say anything.

"That is the story about the creation of Mammoth
Site's Karst sinkhole," replied Mr. Chisholm. "And
since PaleoJoe is the best story teller I know, why don't
I let him tell this story?"

PaleoJoe smiled. As it happened, this was one of
the stories he liked to tell.

"About 26,000 years ago," he began, folding his
arms across his chest, "there was a limestone cavern
right here where we are standing. Limestone caverns
can sometimes collapse. When they do they can form

a type of sinkhole called *karst*. That's what happened here. "When the sinkhole was formed it created a vertical shaft called a *breccia* pipe. It made a chimney-like opening for the warm water of an artesian spring to bubble up through the rock. Eventually, the spring created a pond of warm water and vegetation that was surrounded by very steep sides."

"The enticement," said Mr. Chisholm, with a wink at Dakota.

Dakota pretended not to notice. He was getting the idea of enticement just fine now.

"Certainly so," agreed PaleoJoe. "Can you imagine what happened next?"

"The animals came to drink from the pond," said Shelly sounding superior. Dakota rolled his eyes. *As if that was difficult to figure out*, he thought.

"That's it exactly," said PaleoJoe. "The warm water was inviting to drink and bathe in. The vegetation was good to eat and animals, like these mammoths, got into the pond, but because of the steep sides they were unable to get out again."

"Kind of like La Brea tar pits," observed Dakota. "Only without the tar of course."

"It was exactly like that," said Mr. Chisholm.

"When the animals can't get out they die of starvation, exhaustion, or drowning," said Shelly.

"When the water dried up and the sinkhole filled in again, this became their tomb," finished PaleoJoe.

"And one of the greatest fossil treasures we have

71

ever uncovered," added Mr. Chisholm. "Look at this beauty right here for example," he ran his hand over the fossil skull he had been working on. "This is the skull of a Columbian mammoth. Isn't it beautiful?"

"Do the Blue Tusks belong to a woolly or a Columbian mammoth?" asked Dakota.

"Aha!" shouted Mr. Chisholm loud enough that it made Dakota jump. "A true detective, I see! The Blue Tusks belong to a woolly."

"What's the difference between a Columbian mammoth and a woolly?" asked Shelly.

Dakota sighed. Always with Shelly it was the science questions that were important. Didn't anyone care about the idea of the mysterious?

"The Columbian mammoth descended from the ancestral mammoths that crossed the Bering Land Bridge to get into North America," explained Mr. Chisholm. "The Columbian mammoths were—well, mammoth! They stood almost 14 feet high at their shoulder.

"The woolly mammoths were smaller. They were only about eleven feet high at the shoulder. They had large curved tusks. And they were covered in a hairy coat of course, because they lived south of the ice sheets and ranged from northern Europe, across Siberia, and into North America."

"I know about Siberia," Shelly interrupted. "My great Aunt is there right now studying the fossil remains of a woolly rhino."

"A lucky woman," smiled Mr. Chisholm.

As Mr. Chisholm continued with his description of mammoths, Dakota wandered slightly away from the group. Moving behind an outcropping of shelf hid him almost entirely from view.

He felt like he was walking on an alien landscape. Something like Mars maybe. He scrambled over some lower ridges, carefully avoided walking on a delicate ripple of bones, and made his way to the far side of the excavation. A sliver of light in the wall indicated another doorway.

Curious, Dakota made his way over and opened the door. A dimly lit corridor of offices lay just beyond. The main bank of overhead lights was off leaving only some small secondary lights to illuminate the long hallway in an eerie shadowy glow. All the office doors were closed, the windows dark. It was quiet. Everyone had gone home for the evening.

As Dakota turned around to go back into the sinkhole excavation, a muffled crash sounded in one of the nearby offices.

A dark, supposedly locked, and uninhabited office.

CHAPTER THIRTEEN

SPYING

Dakota couldn't resist. He decided to investigate.

Slipping cautiously into the corridor, he closed the door to the pit excavation behind him. He listened carefully. The corridor was deserted. There didn't seem to be anyone else about.

Dakota's sharp eyes spotted one of the office doors slightly ajar. Walking on tiptoe he silently approached.

Holding his breath he listened. Now he could clearly hear the sounds of someone moving around somewhere inside the darkened office.

For a brief moment, Dakota considered going back and getting PaleoJoe and Mr. Chisholm. But was that what Dexter North would do? Someone was in that office and most likely it was someone who shouldn't be. Using his famous sussing techniques, Dexter North would find out who it was and what they were doing.

Slowly and gently, Dakota put pressure on the office door so that it opened just wide enough to allow him to slip inside. Crouching low, Dakota whisked into the room. He froze, back against the wall, ears straining and eyes blinking in the almost total darkness.

Now he could clearly hear the sound of someone moving around. But it didn't sound very close to where he remained crouched against the wall.

Listening carefully, Dakota determined that the office he crouched in must be a sort of outer office to another room further in. From the direction of that other room, Dakota could clearly hear the shuffle and scrape of someone moving.

Squinting through the gloom of the place, Dakota finally spotted a ribbon of darker shadow. A brief flash of light that came at uneven times mysteriously punctuated that dark. Dakota realized that what he was seeing was the edge of another partially open door and the darker room beyond. The light was from a flashlight.

Whoever it was in there was searching for something.

Crawling on his hands and knees Dakota headed for the door. By crawling Dakota thought he could avoid crashing into unexpected things.

It was good thinking.

Almost immediately Dakota encountered a chair. On hands and knees it was easy to avoid with only a minor bash on his forehead. He crawled around it and was immediately swallowed by a small cave.

He had crawled under a desk.

Backing out, Dakota continued his journey across the spooky landscape of a dark, unfamiliar office. The sharp smell of copy ink, and the rough nylon tickle of the carpet made him want to sneeze. He squinted his eyes in determination and crawled onward.

Just beyond the dark hulk of a copy machine, Dakota tangled with the large pot of a massive plant. He could smell the potted dirt. The leaves of whatever plant it was trailed low touching the floor in front of him. It was like suddenly being in a miniature jungle. The spidery leaves tickled as they swung in Dakota's face. The plant seemed to be placed next to the other doorway, just where Dakota himself wanted to be.

Then suddenly, as he was trying to find a way around the jungle plant to get closer to the open door, a light was switched on inside the room. Dakota's heart thumped into his throat.

He froze.

But no one emerged from the now lighted room and Dakota remained undiscovered. Burrowing next to the wall behind the plant, Dakota finally reached the opening of the door. Trying to not breathe for fear of being heard, he crouched near the ribbon of sudden light. A long tendril of leaf from the plant tickled down the back of his neck.

From inside the room, Dakota could hear the sound of drawers being opened and the rustle of papers being thrown onto the floor. There was a thump, like a chair being overturned, and then a ripping sound like paper being torn.

Someone was really ransacking the office. Dakota decided he had to take a quick look to see who was in there. Then he would go and get PaleoJoe.

Moving as slowly as a turtle in a dense jungle, Dakota cautiously peered through the crack of the open door.

In the now brightly lit inner office, Dakota saw the figure of a man, dressed in black, bent over an overturned chair. He was ripping off the fabric under the seat of the chair using a small knife. Around him papers lay strewn across the floor like a square snowfall. It was obvious to Dakota that the man was not the evening custodian emptying garbage and dusting shelves.

Whatever the man was looking for he wasn't finding it. With a low growl of anger, he stabbed the knife into the seat cushion of the chair. There was another ripping sound as foam padding spilled out onto the floor. Then the man straightened up and glared around the room. As he turned fully in the direction of the door, Dakota's eyes went wide in sudden panic and his heart slammed into his ribs like a rampaging dinosaur.

He recognized the man.

It was Buzzsaw.

CHAPTER FOURTEEN

A TERRIBLE THEFT

Buzzsaw.

Dakota's stomach suddenly twisted into what felt like a complicated sailor's knot. During his most recent encounter with this particular bad guy, Dakota had been almost choked to death. He wasn't eager to tangle with Buzzsaw again. It was time to leave and find reinforcements.

Tense with anxiety, Dakota slowly began to back away.

Suddenly Buzzsaw gave a small cry and lunged toward the door. Fear washed over Dakota. He squeezed his eyes shut and braced himself. But the expected pounding of fists, or the clutching of shirtfront, or the hauling into the air by his ear didn't happen.

Dakota opened his eyes. Two inches from his nose was Buzzsaw's pant leg; a brown khaki with grease stains on the tattered cuff. The peculiar sour smell that was part of Buzzsaw invaded Dakota's nose.

Buzzsaw had not spotted him. Instead, Buzzsaw had apparently found what he was looking for. Dakota could tell by the satisfied snorts the evil man was making.

Waiting no longer, Dakota retreated. Still crawling but moving as fast as he could, Dakota made it as far as the desk when the light of the inner office suddenly snapped off. Without even thinking about it, like an ancient trilobite at the sign of danger, Dakota curled into a ball and rolled into the small cave of the desk. He held his breath.

Dakota heard the stealthy tread of footsteps coming closer to where he hid. He could see the zigzag spurts of light from the flashlight as Buzzsaw walked by and made for the outer office door.

Dakota cautiously peered around the base of the desk. He could see Buzzsaw's shadow hulking in the dark and then, suddenly, the dancing pinpoint of light disappeared as Buzzsaw snapped off the flashlight.

Silence invaded the office.

Dakota watched, straining his eyes in the gloom. Then came the small *click* of the office door opening and the *snick* as it softly closed again. The only thing left for Dakota to hear was the thunder of his own heart.

It had been a narrow escape. Dakota waited another minute or two to be sure that Buzzsaw had indeed gone. Finally deciding it was safe to move, Dakota rolled out from under the desk and stood up.

His eyes were adjusted enough to the dark now that he could make out the shadowy humps of furniture. A small square of light from the hallway glowed in the window of the main office door.

Dakota was alone.

Cautiously he approached the door. It wouldn't be a good idea to suddenly burst out into that brightly lit narrow hallway and find himself eye to eye with Buzzsaw.

Slowly he turned the doorknob and made an unwelcome, sudden discovery. The door was locked.

He was locked in!

He thought about banging on the door and yelling. That, however, might attract Buzzsaw. What could he do?

Dakota made his way back into the smaller office where Buzzsaw had been. He turned on the office light. The small office was a mess. Books and papers were dumped on the floor, a small desk lamp was shattered, and the desk chair lay on its side. Buzzsaw had really torn through things to get whatever it was he had been after.

And Dakota had a pretty good idea what that had been.

As Dakota shuffled forward into the mess of

papers on the floor he accidentally kicked up a small plaque buried in the debris. Dakota bent down and picked it up. It was a desk nameplate. It said *Doug Chisholm.*

Now Dakota was convinced. Buzzsaw had been after the monk's journal about the Blue Tusks. And Dakota was fairly certain Buzzsaw had found it.

Dakota whipped out his cell phone. He punched in a number. The phone buzzed in his ear.

"Dakota?" It was Shelly. Her voice sounded like it was coming from somewhere in China.

"Shelly," said Dakota and found his voice was hoarse with the tension he felt.

"Where are you? We've been looking everywhere for you. PaleoJoe is starting to get a little grumpy and I can't tell you how embarrassed I am about all this. I think Mr. Chisholm thinks there might be something wrong with you. Mentally I mean."

"Shelly!" Dakota interrupted her jabber. "Listen. You have to be careful. Something very bad is happening…"

"I quite agree," said a cold and hostile voice from the doorway.

CHAPTER FIFTEEN

GETTING THE POINT

Dakota spun around and found himself face to face with a woman who looked like she had been eating something extremely sour. Her gray hair, pulled back in a bun so tight, looked like it was stretching the sides of her face.

She glared at Dakota out of black-rimmed glasses perched on the end of her long, sharp nose. Loops of the chain of her eyeglass holders tapped her artificially reddened cheeks. She wore a gray skirt, a white blouse, and dangerous looking square black shoes.

She was also holding a long and evil looking spear. It was pointed at Dakota's heart.

"Step away from the desk you hooligan," she said, "or I will impale you like a shish-ka-bob."

"Uh...talk to you later, Shelly," Dakota muttered. He flipped his phone closed, raised his hands over his head and stepped away from the desk. It was just like how the bad guys in a Dexter North show always raised their hands; only Dakota doubted any of them had ever been menaced by a spear held by someone's grandmother.

"This isn't what it looks like," said Dakota to the woman.

"Never mind about that," said the woman shaking the spear in a threatening manner. "Just don't try any shenanigans. Mr. Chisholm is on his way. He knows how to deal with young yahoots like yourself."

The woman glared at Dakota. Dakota tried to defend himself by producing his famous I'm-So-Totally-Innocent look—the one that made moms want to hug him. It didn't work.

"What's all this then, Mrs. Muhler?" Doug Chisholm pushed his way into the office.

"I found this yahoot ransacking your office, Doug," said the woman. "Just give me the word and I'll skewer him for you."

She faked a lunge at Dakota that made him jump.

Mr. Chisholm pushed past the lady with the deadly spear and stopped short when he saw the destruction of his office. Dakota watched with a sinking feeling as Mr. Chisholm's face scrunched in anger. An anger that was immediately directed at Dakota.

"This is a terrible destruction, young man," Mr. Chisholm thundered shaking his fist in Dakota's face. "I don't care if you are with PaleoJoe. I will not hesitate to press charges."

"But..." Dakota tried to explain.

"Who do you think you are, breaking into my office like this?" Mr. Chisholm wouldn't listen. "You are nothing more than a juvenile delinquent. Is this how you repay PaleoJoe for bringing you along on this tour? I will inform your parents as well as the authorities and I will expect you to pay for all damages."

"Exactly right," said Mrs. Muhler. She had not lowered her spear.

Dakota, close to tears of anger and frustration, felt like running but he didn't see how he could get past the spear wielding Mrs. Muhler.

"Stop! Dakota didn't do this." A fierce figure with a dancing red ponytail suddenly pushed her way past Mrs. Muhler and came to stand by Dakota.

It was Shelly.

She stormed into the room like a small thunderstorm angrily facing Mr. Chisholm, her hands on her hips.

"Tell them, Dakota," she demanded.

Dakota felt a sudden surge of gratitude toward Shelly. He wasn't alone in this. "I didn't..." Dakota tried to explain.

"That's right," Shelly interrupted. "You didn't. Mr. Chisholm, shame on you for jumping to conclusions without hearing his side of the story. Apologize at once."

Mr. Chisholm glared from Shelly to Dakota not knowing which one to tackle first. Just then PaleoJoe arrived guiding Mr. Zephaniah.

"Dakota," exclaimed PaleoJoe pushing his way into the destruction of the room. "Are you all right?"

Dakota felt his anger drain away. Shelly had stood up for him and now PaleoJoe had recognized that danger had been present and that he, Dakota, had been in the path of it.

"PaleoJoe, it was Buzzsaw," said Dakota quickly.

"Buzzsaw!" exclaimed Shelly in dismay.

"I think he stole your journal, Mr. Chisholm," said Dakota.

"Oh no," Mr. Chisholm marched to the bookcase by the door. "He's right, PaleoJoe. The journal of the Blue Tusks is gone."

"Gone?" Mrs. Muhler advanced a step and, for a minute, it looked to Dakota like she was going to attack the bookcase with her spear. "I wouldn't be so quick to let this yahoot off the hook, Mr. Chisholm. How do we know he didn't take it?"

"Because he didn't," said Shelly, scowling at Mrs. Muhler. "And where do you think we are anyway, the African jungle? You could hurt someone with that spear."

"Put the spear down, Daisy," said Mr. Chisholm.

85

Reluctantly, Daisy Muhler lowered her spear, which had, had Shelly only known it, actually come from an obscure tribe in South Africa. The chief had presented it to Mrs. Muhler on one of her long ago expeditions.

"I'm afraid if the journal is gone, so is any possibility of finding the Blue Tusks," said Mr. Chisholm. "All the details were in it."

"Can you remember any of them?" asked Mr. Zephaniah anxiously. "Was there a map?"

"There was no map," Mr. Chisholm shook his head. "But there was detailed descriptions of the landscape with certain landmarks indicated. I can't remember all of them. There was a great deal about hills and rocky places. I feel sure that if someone had the journal they would have a good chance of figuring out exactly where the Tusks are hidden."

"Well, Buzzsaw has that information now," said Dakota.

"I'm sure he doesn't plan on doing anything good with it either," said Shelly.

"Who is this Buzzsaw character?" asked Mr. Zephaniah.

"A former graduate student of mine," said PaleoJoe. "His real name is…"

"Wait, let me guess," interrupted Mr. Zephaniah. He had a strange sinking feeling in the pit of his stomach. "Theodore Edward Kaskia III?"

CHAPTER SIXTEEN

THE BLUE PENDANT

"That's him," nodded PaleoJoe.

"How did you know?" asked Dakota.

"Theodore Edward Kaskia the third is the man I've been looking for," said Mr. Zephaniah. "I think he is the leader of that new group of fossil smugglers I told you about."

"That sounds like him," muttered Dakota.

"But how could he know?" asked Shelly in frustration. "It's like he's a mind reader or something."

"I'm afraid it isn't all that mysterious," said Mr. Chisholm. "The find of the journal was in the local papers all last week. They even ran a story on the history of the Blue Tusks."

"Anyone on the lookout for that sort of thing would have been immediately interested," said PaleoJoe.

"Well," said Mr. Zephaniah, trying to keep the edge of disappointment out of his voice, "I guess that's that. There is no way of finding the Blue Tusks, or even determining if they exist, without the journal."

"Well Buzzsaw must believe that they exist otherwise he wouldn't have bothered stealing it," Dakota pointed out.

"Bother that Buzzsaw!" Shelly exclaimed. "We have to stop him, PaleoJoe."

PaleoJoe scratched his beard thoughtfully. "How authentic do you think that journal was, Doug?"

"Oh, I think it was real all right," said Mr. Chisholm. "It was written by Bernard Falen, who was a lay brother of the Cistercian monks. He writes about finding the tusks. He describes them in very specific detail. And then he talks about having to hide them to keep them safe until he has a chance to get them back to his Abbey."

"Did the journal state specifically where Bernard Falen hid the tusks?" asked PaleoJoe.

"Not real specifically," said Mr. Chisholm. "Apparently Barnard Falen discovered the Blue Tusks on the Taimyr Peninsula of Siberia. He could not keep the discovery a secret and there were many people after him to get the Tusks. He had to hide them quickly so, apparently, it was somewhere close to where he discovered them."

"Siberia is a big place," Shelly piped in. "My Great Aunt Felicia is doing research there. She says that…"

PaleoJoe held up his hand for silence. "Could we leave your great aunt out of this for a minute, please Shelly?" He was feeling a headache coming on.

Shelly frowned, but she stopped babbling. That made Dakota happy, too.

"It would seem logical that the Bernard fellow found the tusks in Siberia," said Mr. Zephaniah. "There are a lot of mammoth remains on the Siberian Steppes. In the summer they thaw out of the frozen tundra. Many of the nomads who live there can make a good profit selling mammoth ivory."

"Who buys mammoth ivory?" asked Dakota.

"Ever since the ban on elephant ivory went into effect, traders and sellers of all sorts have been after mammoth ivory," said PaleoJoe. "There is a trade in items made of ivory. Not only that, but there is also a large demand for ivory that has been ground up."

"What is that for?" asked Dakota.

"Some people take it like medicine," explained PaleoJoe.

"That would be yuck," said Dakota. "I think I'll stick to chicken noodle soup and beef jerky." Whenever Dakota got a cold his mother made him chicken noodle soup and Dakota was convinced that beef jerky was the perfect food—good for whatever a person might suffer from.

"Why didn't that Bernard fellow leave a map?" asked Shelly. "How can anyone be expected to find something in as gigantic a place as Siberia without a map?"

"There was no map in the journal," said Mr. Chisholm. "I think the only lead we had was the description Bernard Falen wrote of the rivers and natural landscape. Without the journal we have nothing."

"Of course there is still the pendant," said Mrs. Muhler suddenly. "That Buzzsaw yahoot didn't get that because I'm wearing it."

"Oh yes," said Mr. Chisholm snapping his fingers. "I had forgotten about that. But I don't think the pendant is anything that can help us much, Daisy. I think it is only decorative."

Mrs. Muhler, leaning on her spear, shrugged her bony shoulders. "The secret societies of some African tribes hide their knowledge in a coded language that looks, to the uninitiated, like the decorative design on pots. It's just a thought," she said. "But here—you can see for yourself."

From around her neck Mrs. Muhler unfastened a slender silver chain. Attached to the chain was a delicate blue pendant in the shape of the head of a deer.

"You never know about treasure," she said. "Sometimes the most valuable things are right there under your nose."

CHAPTER SEVENTEEN

A PRETTY TRINKET

Mrs. Muhler handed the blue pendant to Shelly.

"It's beautiful," whispered Shelly, carefully holding the small, blue object up to the light.

Dakota, uncertain he knew much about beauty, had to agree that what Shelly gently clasped between her finger and thumb looked quite special. The object was a small carving of the head of a deer whose antlers swept back in graceful curves like the curl of blue waves. It was a pretty, sky blue and looked like stone.

"What is it?" he asked.

"It's a pendant," said Shelly. "Like for a necklace."

"Yes, I can see that, Ms. Obvious," said Dakota. "What I mean is, what is it a shape of? Is it a deer head?"

"Is it odontolite?" asked PaleoJoe, getting out his loupe for a closer look.

"It is a piece of odontolite," said Mr. Chisholm. "I think that maybe it is carved from a bit of the Blue Tusks themselves. It was hidden in the back of the journal, glued between two pieces of parchment. I don't think it is anything more than a pretty trinket."

"But why would Bernard Falen go to such trouble to hide it in his journal if it was just a pretty trinket?" asked Shelly.

"Maybe it was proof of the Blue Tusks," said Mr. Chisholm.

Dakota shook his head. "That doesn't sound right to me," he said. "There has to be more to it than that."

"Wishful thinking, young man," said Mr. Chisholm.

"May I see it?" asked Mr. Zephaniah, holding out his hand. Carefully PaleoJoe placed the pendant in his palm.

Mr. Zephaniah ran the tips of his fingers gently over the surface of the pendant. As he did, a smile began to wiggle the gray mustache on his upper lip.

"This is truly remarkable," he said.

"It's very pretty," said Shelly, "but how is it remarkable?"

"Oh, this is more than a pretty trinket, Shelly," said Mr. Zephaniah now grinning widely. "Much more."

"What is it then?" asked Dakota.

"It's a map!" said Mr. Zephaniah.

"How can that be?" asked Mr. Chisholm.

"Wait," said Shelly breathlessly. "PaleoJoe, may I borrow your loupe?"

PaleoJoe handed Shelly his small, powerful magnifying glass. "Let me see, Mr. Zephaniah," she said. For a long moment Shelly intently studied the carving.

"What do you see?" asked Mr. Zephaniah.

"I'm not sure," said Shelly wrinkling her forehead in concentration. "There are markings of some sort carved onto the surface but I think they must be just scratches, Mr. Zephaniah."

"Let me see," said Dakota. Shelly handed him the carving and the loupe. In the bubble-like magnification of the blue surface of the carving, Dakota could easily make out the minute scratches Shelly had found.

"The question I have," said Dakota, "is why is this pendant in the shape of a deer head?"

"Hmmm," said Mr. Chisholm thinking. "I don't know."

"I think I do," said Mrs. Muhler unexpectedly. "Anthropology is my specialty," she explained as everyone gave her a surprised look. "I know a thing or two and I can tell you if you want to hear about it."

"Please tell us," said Shelly. And then to Dakota, "Anthropology is the study of people in case you are wondering."

"I wasn't," he informed her.

93

Mrs. Muhler grinned. It made her face seem more skull-like then ever, thought Dakota nervously. Still, now that she wasn't waving a deadly spear around in the air she seemed quite nice.

"I don't think that pendant is carved in the shape of a deer head," Mrs. Muhler began. "Or rather it is a deer, but a special kind of deer. I think it is a reindeer. And I think that because I happen to know that on the Taimyr Peninsula there is a group of reindeer herders known as the Dolgan. They are a nomadic group of people who follow the migration of their reindeer herds.

"The Dolgan," continued Mrs. Muhler, "have been known to frequently find and sell or trade pieces of mammoth tusks that melt out of the tundra on the Taimyr Peninsula."

"You think these Dolgan might know where the Blue Tusks are hidden?" asked Shelly.

"No," said Mr. Zephaniah. "I for one don't think that would be the case, because if they had found the tusks I think they would have sold them a long time ago."

Mrs. Muhler nodded. "I think that would be right."

"So what then?" asked Shelly.

Dakota couldn't help feeling a wave of smugness as he realized that he was working this out before Shelly.

"Shelly, I don't think those scratches are random,"

he said. "I think they were made deliberately and Mr. Zephaniah is right. It's a map of the Taimyr Peninsula and it will tell us where the Blue Tusks are hidden."

CHAPTER EIGHTEEN

The Map

There was a moment of silence in the room as everyone considered this.

"Well, there's one way to find out," said Mrs. Muhler. "Follow me." And hefting her spear over her shoulder like a hunter in the jungle, and almost poking PaleoJoe in the eye in the process, she led the way out of Mr. Chisholm's office.

Back into the corridor they went, down two doors and then Mrs. Muhler ushered the group into another office. Her office.

It was the coolest office Dakota had ever seen. It was filled with skulls—human skulls—and pieces of pottery. Tatters of odd-looking tapestries hung from the walls. There were other things too—like spears. Lots of spears. Mrs. Muhler had a whole collection of spears and they were arranged in brackets on the wall. One of the brackets was empty. Mrs. Muhler marched over and replaced the spear she was carrying.

"Sorry about threatening to make you into a shish-ka-bob," she said as she noticed Dakota watching her. "Only you understand, I thought you were a yahoot."

"I understand," said Dakota. "Only I'm not, you know."

"That's good," Mrs. Muhler gave Dakota a big smile. "I wouldn't like to be friends with a yahoot."

Dakota grinned back.

"Now then, look at this everybody," said Mrs. Muhler marching over to a cabinet of long shallow drawers. Pulling one open, she took out a large flat sheet of paper. When the paper was spread out on Mrs. Muhler's worktable, Shelly could see that it was a map of Siberia.

"Oh look," she said, leaning over the map excitedly and stabbing at it with her finger. "It's right here, somewhere east of this river right here. That's where my Great Aunt Felicia is doing her research. Her team is excavating a woolly rhino and it's the coolest thing. I just got a letter from her last week and she told me all about how cool—and cold—their campsite is. I can't imagine what it is like. She says that in winter your breath actually freezes solid in the air right in front of your face. How could that be? Wouldn't you run into your own breath? You could hurt yourself…"

"Shelly Brooks," said PaleoJoe in a rather loud voice. "Please disengage Chatter Mode."

"Oh, sorry," said Shelly, but she continued to pour over the map.

"Here is the Taimyr Peninsula," said Mrs. Muhler, tracing her finger over an area on the upper region of what, to Dakota, looked like the biggest continent he had ever seen.

Maybe the map is drawn to a super large scale, he thought. But another part of his mind told him that wasn't the case. Siberia was a very big place.

"Malachi, if you can make a sketch of the scratches on the pendant," said PaleoJoe, "we can see if they match this map at all."

"Brilliant," said Dakota.

Mrs. Muhler provided some paper and a pencil. As though touching something very delicate, Mr. Zephaniah ran his finger tips lightly over the pendant feeling the faint scratches on the surface of it. Then he began to draw what his fingertips were "seeing."

It didn't take him long before he had drawn something that looked, to Dakota, a lot like a map.

They all bent closer to study it.

"Yes," said Mr. Chisholm excitedly. "Look here. This line matches this river here. And this ripple could indicate this shoreline. I don't know. What do you think, PaleoJoe?"

PaleoJoe frowned as he studied the drawing. "I think that it is almost an unbelievable thing if this is just coincidence," he said.

"Look," said Shelly. "See right here where these lines make a patch? What do you think that is?"

"I think it is X," said Dakota. "As in X marks the spot."

"X marks the spot," muttered PaleoJoe thoughtfully. "I think that's right, Dakota." And then he burst out in a roaring laugh. "Jumping *Velociraptor*, Malachi! I think you have found the location of the Blue Tusks!"

Mr. Zephaniah laughed too, and Mr. Chisholm and Mrs. Muhler joined in. Shelly punched Dakota on the arm and Dakota pounded on her back.

"Now PaleoJoe," said Mr. Zephaniah. "All we need is someone to go and find them."

PaleoJoe nodded and his eyes gleamed with the thought of such an adventure. *I will have to get special permission from Mrs. Pengelly,* his thoughts raced ahead. *I've spent my travel budget but surely she would allow me some funds to go in search of such fabulous fossils as the Blue Tusks!*

"Wow," said Shelly looking in amazement at one of the biggest landmasses on the planet. It was unbelievable that she was actually going to have the chance to see it.

"Dakota, we're going to Siberia!" she whooped and gave Dakota a high five.

"Yes!" Dakota pounded fists with her.

"Well, don't get carried away here, you two,"

99

said PaleoJoe. "I'm going to Siberia. You are not. With Buzzsaw on the loose this mission is much too dangerous."

"Hog wash," said Mrs. Muhler looking intently at her collection of spears.

But because PaleoJoe was looking at the map he didn't see the spark of anger flare in Shelly's eyes or the determined set of her mouth. He didn't see Mrs. Muhler wink at Shelly. He didn't know that Mr. Zephaniah gave Shelly's elbow a squeeze of encouragement.

Dakota, however, did not miss any of it. He flipped to a new page in his notebook and began making a list of the stuff he wanted to pack for a trip to Siberia.

SIBERIA EXPEDITION

1. Buy a warm hat

2. Beef Jerky

CHAPTER NINETEEN

A BUG AND A BRIBE

"No," said PaleoJoe as he took three large steps to get ahead of Shelly.

"Yes!" Shelly gave a skip and a hop, which easily caught her up to him.

"Absolutely not, and that is final," growled PaleoJoe, dodging into the crowd on the main floor of the Balboa, thinking that would separate him from Shelly.

He was wrong.

"PaleoJoe, please stop arguing and take this with you." Shelly had easily kept up with him and now he felt her shove something into his back pocket. He stopped and glared down at his red pony-tailed tormentor.

"Pish!" he scowled. "I will not stoop to bribery."

He reached into his back pocket and extracted a large candy bar in a bright gold foil wrap. It was a ChocoDelight Bar, special dark chocolate with hazelnuts. They were sold at the Balboa coffee shop and, according to Shelly, it was Mrs. Pengelly's favorite.

"Look, PaleoJoe," said Shelly with a huge effort at being patient. "You need to ask Mrs. Pengelly for money to travel to Siberia to look for those tusks. You have already spent your travel budget..."

"I've spent over my travel budget," PaleoJoe interrupted.

"Even worse," said Shelly. "You will need something to sweeten her up."

"It won't work," said PaleoJoe as he tried to give the candy bar back to Shelly.

"Miles says it's her very favorite," said Shelly refusing to take it. "Try it. You'll need everything you can use on this one, PaleoJoe. It will take a lot of money to get us to Siberia."

"To get me to Siberia," PaleoJoe corrected her. "You're not going."

"Of course not," said Shelly in the same overly calm voice she used on Miles when he had a temper outburst. "But just try, okay?"

They had reached the museum offices now and PaleoJoe looked even gloomier than before. Without another word he shoved the candy bar back into his pocket and knocked on the museum director's office door.

"Come in, PaleoJoe," Mrs. Pengelly called.

"Good luck," said Shelly, giving a perky thumbs-up sign. PaleoJoe gave her a sour look and walked into Mrs. Pengelly's office closing the door behind him.

Shelly found a seat on a bench in the short hall outside Mrs. Pengelly's office and sat down to wait. She felt nervous. She looked at her watch. It was 1:00. According to their daring and elaborate plan, Gamma Brooks would be along in about 10 minutes. Shelly whipped out her pink space-age cell phone and punched in Dakota's number.

"Hey," Dakota answered on the first ring.

"What are you doing?" asked Shelly.

"Packing." Dakota sounded like he was talking in a tin can. Shelly knew it was due to his cheap phone, not hers. "Everything okay?"

"PaleoJoe is talking with Mrs. Pengelly. Gamma should be here any minute. You really think this will work?"

"Of course it will," said Dakota sounding like he had just stuffed his head into a pillow. "Even Mr. Zephaniah thought so."

"I'm glad he's on our side," said Shelly.

Yesterday, after their return from Mammoth Site, Shelly had had a long, private discussion with Mr. Zephaniah.

"It's anyone's guess if this Buzzsaw character will go after the tusks himself or send someone else," Mr. Zephaniah had told her. "I'm heading straight back to work myself. I am determined to break up

103

this new organization."

"And put a stop to their nefarious deeds," said Shelly, using one of her favorite words.

Mr. Zephaniah had nodded his head in agreement. "I think PaleoJoe could use you and Mr. Jackson on this adventure. You two are sharp thinkers and you could help him."

"You mean we can wrestle grizzlies," said Shelly.

"Absolutely!" Mr. Zephaniah grinned at her.

"Don't worry," Shelly had assured him. "I'm thinking of a plan. We will all three be going to Siberia!"

And it had, as usual, been her Gamma Brooks who had helped her devise a scheme.

"Here I am, Pepperpie," said Gamma Brooks, as she suddenly appeared waving at Shelly.

"Here's Gamma now," Shelly said into her phone. "I'll call you when we finish."

"Good luck," said Dakota and hung up.

"Well, here it is," said Gamma, plopping herself down on the bench next to her granddaughter. She was holding a small wooden box with a glass cover. Inside, on a fluffy white pillow of backing, was a small black bug.

"*Grylloblattodea* or ice bug," said Gamma Brooks proudly. "From the Greek *gryll*, which means 'cricket' and *blatta* which means 'cockroach.' Only 25 species have ever been described in the entire world. It is an ancient and primitive insect. They are only found in very cold parts of the world. This one was found in Siberia by your Great Aunt Felicia. Are you ready, Cricketeer?"

Shelly nodded and stood up. With a proud smile at her insect, Gamma Brooks, amateur entomologist and co-conspirator, marched up to Mrs. Pengelly's door and demonstrated her skill at one of her granddaughter's favorite pastimes: barging.

A quick rap at the door and, without waiting for an answer, Gamma pushed her way inside with Shelly close on her heels.

"Mrs. Pengelly, I'm so happy to catch you at your desk," said Gamma in a loud, cheerful voice as she entered the office.

Shelly noticed the ChocoDelight bar shining in its gold wrapper on the edge of Mrs. Pengelly's desk. PaleoJoe scowled at the interruption and then turned red when he saw Shelly spy the candy bar. Shelly grinned at him and waggled her fingers in a quick wave.

"Pish," said PaleoJoe, but he mumbled it in his beard and no one really heard him.

"Here is that rare specimen my sister just sent me," said Gamma plopping the bug down on Mrs. Pengelly's desk.

"Oh, it's very interesting, just as you said, Mrs. Brooks," said Mrs. Pengelly, enthusiastically picking up the case for a closer look. "We are very lucky to have your sister donating such valuable additions to our collections. I'm glad we have the chance to return the favor."

"Mrs. Brooks," said PaleoJoe. "I'm afraid we are right in the middle of a discussion here. If you could just wait a minute, I'll get through and you…"

"Oh don't worry, PaleoJoe," said Gamma. "I'm sure that Mrs. Pengelly will allow you to accompany Shelly and Dakota. In fact, my sister requested it specifically."

"Accompany Shelly and Dakota where?" PaleoJoe frowned, puzzled. "Your sister?"

"Yes, PaleoJoe," said Mrs. Pengelly. "I think you met Felicia Benton when she was in the museum last summer."

PaleoJoe nodded. Sometimes he felt as though he were caught in a high wind and had lost his sense of direction when he was with Gamma Brooks. And when she was with Shelly, he reflected, the combination could be deadly.

"Well, Ms. Benton is in the middle of digging an almost fully preserved Woolly Rhino."

"Yes, I've heard something about that," said PaleoJoe with a suspicious glance at Shelly.

"And she has requested that you and the kids be allowed to join her for a few days, lending your expertise on the dig site. I'm afraid you will have to drop whatever it is you are doing just now, but it can't be helped. You will have to leave immediately because, of course, the weather is closing in. They have such short warm seasons, you know."

PaleoJoe was confused. "Ummm…" he said.

"Oh, of course the museum will fund your travel, even though you are over your budget. This little fellow right here," she gestured to the bug, "is worth it all by himself. Very rare," Mrs. Pengelly paused for breath and noticed the confused look on PaleoJoe's face, which had also gone pale because of a thought that had just occurred to him.

The thought was that Shelly had made a Plan and he was about to be caught in it.

"What's wrong, PaleoJoe?"

"Nothing, Mrs. Pengelly," said PaleoJoe, wishing he had a strong cup of coffee to clear the fog rolling in his head. He glanced at Shelly who seemed to be absorbed in looking at the bug on Mrs. Pengelly's desk. "It's just that right now, as I was trying to tell you, I have an important request to make…"

"Better tell him where the dig is, Mrs. Pengelly," said Shelly.

"Oh, didn't I say?" Mrs. Pengelly fluttered a hand in the air. "Ms. Benton's crew is near the Khatanga River in northern Siberia. It's on the Taimyr Peninsula. Have you heard of it?"

"Yes," said PaleoJoe feeling a strange and numb calm invade his body. He stared at a point on the ceiling just above Mrs. Pengelly's head. "I have definitely heard of it. I think I had better go pack." And without another word PaleoJoe stood up and walked quietly out of Mrs. Pengelly's office.

"Thanks for the candy bar!" Mrs. Pengelly called after him. "He's such a thoughtful person," she said to Gamma. "How did he know ChocoDelight was my favorite?"

Shelly smiled.

CHAPTER TWENTY

DEEP FREEZE

It was cold in Khatanga. Really cold.

Dakota was shivering in his two pairs of long underwear, turtleneck sweater, flannel shirt, snow pants over jeans, and down jacket that reached to his knees, borrowed from his friend Detective Franks. The only thing that was sort of warm on Dakota was his head and that was thanks to Detective Franks's gift of a real ushanka, the furry Russian hat with the large flaps that covered his ears.

"Dakota," said Shelly walking next to him, "you can stop shivering now. We're inside."

"Yes, inside a giant freezer," Dakota pointed out, his breath making large explosions of white puffs in front of his face.

"It's five degrees in here," said Shelly. "Almost tropic." She laughed at her exaggeration. "And there is no wind. You're shaking like a miniature earthquake and I can hear your teeth chattering."

Dakota scowled. Of course his teeth were chattering. He was cold.

Shelly, in the week before this expedition, had gone shopping with her Gamma Brooks for the appropriate outfit for arctic weather—inside or outside. Unlike Dakota who had had to scrounge in the Goodwill store and borrow from Detective Franks for his arctic attire, Shelly was happily warm in her brand new, hi-tech, insulated pink snowsuit, white fur-lined boots, and matching pink fur cap with the cute pink pom-pom on top.

"Hurry up you two," said PaleoJoe as he disappeared around a bend in the tunnel ahead.

Shelly and Dakota scooted to catch up.

They were inside a cold storage facility in the Russian town of Khatanga. Carved out of the permafrost, the tunnels of this facility stored the small town's winter meat. Shelly and Dakota were passing stacks of frozen silvery fish that lined the walls of the tunnel.

And somewhere in here, as well, were the frozen remains of the woolly rhino Shelly's Great Aunt Felicia Benton and her team had excavated.

As Shelly and Dakota turned a bend in the tunnel following PaleoJoe, brighter lights shone ahead. Dakota could hear a babble of excited voices. And then suddenly they found themselves in a larger room filled with people.

In the center of this cold storage room was a large chunk of frozen tundra about the size of a large pick-up truck. Lights were placed strategically to illuminate the top and sides of the chunk. People were gathered around it, engaged in all sorts of scientific study. Several people were using small picks and brushes. They were examining portions of the chunk of frozen material. Two people were even sprawled on their stomachs, on top of the chunk, using what looked like hair dryers to melt the ice.

As they entered the room, a commotion of people calling out greetings overwhelmed Dakota. He stepped to the side as several people rushed forward. These people were the international team of scientists working with Shelly's great aunt. PaleoJoe called out return greetings and shook hands with people he obviously knew. Shelly found herself scooped up and squeezed in a bear hug by her Great Aunt Felicia.

"Shellybean! It's wonderful to see you!" Shelly's Great Aunt Felicia was younger and shorter than Gamma Brooks and she had only one pet name for Shelly. "Look at how you are growing!" she exclaimed.

Aunt Felicia was always saying that, but now Shelly could see that there was some truth to the comment. Shelly stood eye to twinkling eye with her great aunt. Dressed in a pair of brown, hooded coveralls, Felicia Benton looked perfectly at home in the frozen room. Her breath gushed out in white plumes as she chattered with Shelly. Shelly grinned and hugged back.

"Aunt Felicia, thanks for helping us get to Siberia," said Shelly. Shelly always called her great aunt just simply 'Aunt Felicia.' The two had worked this out between them a long time ago. Great Aunt Felicia would confine herself to one pet name for Shelly and Shelly would call her Aunt instead of Great Aunt.

"I am happy to help," said Aunt Felicia with a sly wink at PaleoJoe.

Dakota stood off to one side momentarily forgotten in the flurry of hugs and hand shakes. As he leaned, shivering, against the wall he noticed a large man whose long, thin face was hidden in a dark tangle of beard and long hair. The man had moved to stand closer to PaleoJoe and it was obvious that he was listening in to the conversation.

Suddenly Dakota's attention was distracted by the appearance of a small dog that danced and yapped merrily around the ankles of the new arrivals. Dakota looked in amazement at the little animal. It was a poodle. A little black poodle and even though she wore a warm looking red plaid coat and little red boots on her feet, a poodle was the last kind of dog one would expect to find in the high arctic.

Dakota watched the happy little dog scooting about making friends with first, PaleoJoe and then, Shelly.

"Her name is Nadezhda," said Aunt Felicia. "It means 'Hope.' But I just call her Sadie. She doesn't seem to mind."

Sadie danced away from Shelly and headed over to Dakota to get acquainted. But in order to get to him, she had to pass by the listening man. There was a quick moment when Dakota saw the little dog hesitate and flinch away from the big booted feet of the man before she quickly scampered past him to get to Dakota.

I don't think she likes that guy, thought Dakota, as he knelt down to pet the dog. *I wonder why.*

CHAPTER TWENTY-ONE

OLD BRUNO

"Is she your dog, Aunt Felicia?" asked Shelly.

Dakota scooped Sadie into his arms, where she wiggled happily and licked his face.

"Sadie showed up with Bruno Kincaid, the mammoth hunter who found our woolly rhino," said Aunt Felicia. "When Bruno disappeared back to the tundra, Sadie stayed. I don't think she really belongs to anyone. My theory is that she just attaches herself to whatever group of humans she finds most interesting. Bruno Kincaid was the most recent."

"Who is Bruno Kincaid?" asked PaleoJoe.

"He's rather a mysterious man," said Aunt Felicia. "He's an old hunter and lives with the nomads, a group of the Dolgans I think, out on the tundra. He makes a pretty good living finding and selling fossil ivory. Anyway that's what he was looking for when he found our rhino."

"But Sadie isn't his dog?" questioned Shelly.

Aunt Felicia shook her head. "Folks around here say not. Sadie attaches herself to groups going out onto the tundra. You would never expect a poodle to love the arctic, but that little gal really does. And she's smart too. She knows when storms are coming, she can tell where the ground is unsafe and she even helped find Old Bruno here. That's what we named the rhino—after Bruno Kincaid."

With a wave of her hand, Aunt Felicia indicated the massive chunk of frozen ground that took up a lot of the interior of the room.

"Truly impressive," said PaleoJoe nodding his head. "How much of it do you think is intact?"

"We don't know for sure," said Aunt Felicia. "We are hoping a great deal of it however. As you know, there have been few woolly rhino mummies found. We are hoping this one will be a very important find."

As far as Dakota was concerned, the one thing of interest about the giant block of frozen ground was the huge horn that stuck out about three feet from one corner of the block. Unlike other horns that he had seen on pictures of modern rhinos or on bulls, this horn was flat not rounded. It almost looked like the giant claw of a monster bird.

"I thought mummies were in Egypt," said

Dakota, managing to keep his teeth from chattering as he said this. Holding Sadie helped. The little dog was like a small heater and she seemed to be content to allow Dakota to hold her.

"Of course," said Aunt Felicia, really getting a good look at Dakota for the first time. She tried to keep her face straight as she took in this obviously cold boy, holding a little poodle, wearing a strange combination of clothing.

He looks like a model for a rummage sale, she thought.

"But a mummy is really just a dried out organism," said Shelly.

"That's right," said Aunt Felicia. "And there are many ways to cause that condition. One of those ways is to get yourself buried in the frozen ground of Siberia for thousands of years."

Dakota shuddered. *I'm cold enough for that*, he thought, shivering in his borrowed artic gear.

"We have found some skin and tufts of hair," Aunt Felicia informed PaleoJoe. "There might even be some organs inside the body, as well. If his stomach is there we will be able to find out what he had for his last dinner 30,000 years ago."

PaleoJoe stepped forward to take a closer look at the cube of frozen earth.

"*Coelodonta antiquitatis,*" he said. "The woolly rhino was an herbivore."

"That means that he ate vegetation," Shelly

informed Dakota, just in case he didn't know.

"And of course, that's why I'm on this team," said Aunt Felicia smiling proudly. "I am a paleobotonist."

"Very cool," said Dakota. "I like this horn though. Is there such a thing as a paleohornologist?"

Aunt Felicia laughed. "I don't think so," she said. "Lots of people are intrigued by the horns of woolly rhinos though. During the 19th century people in Russia often found them, but they thought they were claws of giant birds."

"And woolly rhinos, as well as the woolly mammoths, are in those cave paintings in France," said Shelly. "They were drawn by Neanderthals. I saw pictures of them in a book."

"How big will he be when you get him out of this block of ice?" asked Dakota.

"A woolly rhino grew to be about eleven feet in length and he stood six feet tall at his shoulder," said

Aunt Felicia. "We think this is a full grown adult, but we won't know for sure until we chip him out. We want to go slowly. We also found some plant material crushed in the ice."

"That will give you some valuable information about the ecosystem," observed PaleoJoe.

Just then another scientist approached PaleoJoe with warm greetings. The two shook hands and disappeared around the side of the chunk engaged in eager conversation. Shelly followed her aunt around the other side discussing Gamma Brooks and school. Sadie wiggled impatiently and Dakota set her down. She promptly pranced off after Shelly and her aunt leaving Dakota, now forgotten by everyone, standing near the three foot, claw-like horn that stabbed out of the side of the block.

Carefully he reached out his mittened hand to touch it.

"It would be sort of nasty to find that charging down on your backside," said the man Dakota had noticed earlier listening in to their conversation. He was wearing heavy coveralls like most of the scientists in the room. His mane of wild hair snarled around his head as though it had not seen a comb for weeks. Through his thick beard and mustache he smiled down at Dakota. "Strange thing about the horn of the woolly rhino is that it's made out of hair."

"Hair?" asked Dakota.

"Certainly," said the man. "A woolly rhino's

horn is made of empty tubes of keratin, which is the same substance that your hair is made of, densely compressed together."

"C-c-cool," said Dakota unable to suppress a slight teeth chattering.

"Dimitri Markovitch," said the man extending a large mittened hand to Dakota.

"Dakota Jackson," said Dakota shaking, and shaking hands.

"Are you cold, Dakota Jackson?" asked Dimitri Markovitch.

"Yes," said Dakota.

"Well, think how that fella must feel," said Dimitri. "Be glad you aren't trapped in a great big block of ice."

Dakota looked at the sparkling ice crystals that covered the walls around him and wondered what made Dimitri Markovitch think that they weren't in a great big block of ice.

"Besides," said the man. "It's going to get a lot colder where we are going."

"Where we are going?" asked Dakota confused.

"Yes, I've volunteered to guide you all out onto the tundra to look for those mammoth tusks of yours. What's so special about a pair of mammoth tusks that you people would risk the bad weather of the season's close?"

Dimitri asked the question as though he was just curious, but Dakota remembered how Sadie had acted

119

around the big man and he felt uneasy.

"You'd have to ask PaleoJoe," said Dakota. "I'm just along for the ride."

Dimitri Markovitch stared at him a moment and then he smiled. "I know the feeling," he said.

CHAPTER TWENTY-TWO

A SECRET ESCAPES

"Dakota, why do you always have to be carrying odd things with you?" asked Shelly. Dakota, as usual, was trying his best to be an embarrassment. Shelly suspected he did it on purpose, just to annoy her.

Dressed in her pink coordinating polar outfit, and carrying her pink backpack, she felt mismatched walking next to Dakota's hodgepodge appearance. And this morning he had strapped a board to his back, which was making him look a little stranger than usual.

"What odd things?" asked Dakota, puzzled. The freshly fallen snow squeaked under his boots sounding like Styrofoam, and he was cold. He felt annoyed. Not everyone could afford to look as coordinated as Shelly, even if they wanted to. And even though his down jacket smelled faintly of garlic, he was grateful to Detective Franks for loaning it to him.

"That thing strapped to your back," said Shelly.

"That isn't odd. That's my skateboard," said Dakota. "Only I took off the wheels and added some leather loops to hold my feet on, and now it is my snowboard. I think it's innovative," he said, trying out a vocabulary word his teacher had taught them in their last unit on inventors.

Shelly frowned but just then they passed a group of kids playing by the side of the road. There was a dip in the road, made by ice and some freshly fallen snow of the night before, and the kids were sledding down it on large pieces of cardboard. They whooped and hollered and waved. Shelly smiled and waved back.

"See? Innovation at work," said Dakota.

Shelly gave him a disdainful look and hurried her pace so she would be leading the way, walking in front of Dakota and PaleoJoe.

"PaleoJoe," said Dakota. "Why do we have to have Dimitri Markovitch as our guide?"

They were marching along the street of Khatanga on their way to meet the helicopter that would drop them on the place marked on Mr. Zephaniah's map. Dimitri Markovitch was, just as he had told Dakota, going to be their guide. His work on the rhino was done, he had said, and he would be happy to help PaleoJoe locate the tusks he was after.

Dakota had noticed that PaleoJoe had not told

Dimitri why the tusks were so special. Dakota thought that was a good secret to keep for now.

"He's the best qualified," said PaleoJoe. "And available. Why?"

Dakota shrugged. "I just don't have a good feeling about him."

"Dakota is cold," said Shelly smugly. "He imagines things when his brain freezes."

"Funny," grumbled Dakota. "Why can't we send for that Bruno Kincaid fellow? He's a real mammoth hunter after all. Wouldn't he be the best qualified?"

"We don't have time," said PaleoJoe. "Any day now the weather is going to start to get bad. We don't want to be out on the arctic tundra in any winter storms. Trust me on that."

"At least, let's not tell him why the tusks are special," said Dakota.

"Okay," agreed PaleoJoe. "I think that's probably a good idea anyway. The fewer people who know just what it is we are looking for, the better. After all, we don't know if Buzzsaw is lurking about or not."

Dakota nodded his agreement.

"There's Aunt Felicia!" said Shelly, suddenly waving her hand.

They had come in sight of the gray metal building that served as Khatanga's local airport. Standing out in front were three very different figures: short and stocky Aunt Felicia, tall and hairy Dimitri Markovitch, and small and wiggly Sadie, dressed in

123

her red plaid jacket and boots.

Sadie gave a yip of happy welcome and did a circle dance on her hind legs to show how delighted she was to have her new human friends join her on this expedition, because, as it soon became clear, Sadie was going along too.

Dakota was glad. Dimitri Markovitch made him nervous. Sadie kept him warm.

Aunt Felicia gave Shelly a hug. "Your tents, food, water, and camping gear are loaded on the helicopter," she said. "You have enough supplies for a week, even though you will only be out there for two days. Also, the satellite phone has fresh batteries if you need to contact us before your pick up time. Do you have everything else?"

She looked worriedly at the trio in front of her. Shelly had her back pack, as did PaleoJoe. Aunt Felicia thought they looked ready to go. It was the boy she was worried about. Once again he stood looking colder than the frosted world around him. It had warmed up considerably here in Khatanga, but Aunt Felicia knew the winds on the tundra would make it very cold.

Dakota was dressed all right, she thought, even though he was so mismatched. But all he carried was a duffle bag, and then he had a sled or something slung over his back. She shook her head. Hopefully, PaleoJoe would look after him.

"The helicopter is ready," said Aunt Felicia.

She walked with them through the small building and out onto the paved area in the back. A large orange helicopter stood on the frosted runway, ready for take off. Dakota could see a man in the pilot's seat checking over instruments and preparing to start the engine.

Sadie ran ahead and with a single bound was through the open door at the side of the helicopter. PaleoJoe lifted Shelly in and gave Dakota a leg up. Dimitri gave Aunt Felicia a friendly salute and then folded his large frame inside. He squeezed into the seat next to Dakota.

PaleoJoe turned to shake hands with Aunt Felicia.

"Thanks for all your help," he said.

"Take care," she replied. "I hope you find those blue tusks. What a fantastic thing that will be." She laughed with delight at the thought.

Dakota felt his heart give a quick thump at her words. He glanced quickly at Dimitri to see if he had overheard.

He had.

PaleoJoe climbed into the helicopter and pulled the door closed. He settled himself in the seat next to the pilot who began to flip switches.

"So you're looking for the famous Blue Tusks," said Dimitri Markovitch to Dakota with a thoughtful look on his face. "Of course some people believe they are cursed and will bring death to anyone who disturbs them. If they exist at all," he added as the helicopter roared to life and lurched them into the cold skies of Siberia.

125

CHAPTER TWENTY-THREE

A Discovery

The helicopter ride to the map location took three hours. Dakota looked out the small round window as they flew over Lake Taimyr, its black ice fissured with cracks. Small brown fisherman shacks were like little bumpy pimples on the glass-smooth surface.

Then the tundra came into view and the treeless landscape rolled away beneath the whirling blades of the helicopter. The whop-whop-whop made a lonely noise in the silence of the land below them. They flew over treeless hills marked with bluish shadows of snow. Ice packed rivers made silver ribbons reflecting the sun. Small lakes were mirrors that dotted the white land. Herds of reindeer were everywhere, moving like schools of fish across the frozen tundra in a tightly packed mob.

At least it's warm in here, thought Dakota, trying not to worry that their secret was out. Dimitri now knew exactly what it was they were after.

At last the journey ended and the pilot set them down. PaleoJoe and Dimitri unloaded the supplies and the helicopter roared off leaving the group alone on the vast tundra hundreds of miles from anything.

Cheerfully, Dimitri showed Shelly how to set up the tent and Dakota helped PaleoJoe sort out their equipment.

"We will only have two days to scout for the tusks," said PaleoJoe as they worked. "The weather is supposed to get bad by the end of the week so we don't have much time."

Dakota looked around at the empty land stretching as far as the eye could see. A light dusting of snow whirled into the air making sparkling crystals.

"Where do we start?" he asked.

"We will hike over to those hills," said Dimitri as he joined them. "According to your map, the tusks you are looking for could be anywhere in this area. But I think the most logical place to look would be in a place where there might be a cliff or cavern. After all, they are probably not going to be found just laying on top of the ground."

It was a plan and so, after they had made camp, they set off. It was fifteen degrees and the sky was sunny.

"Hey Dakota," said Shelly as they walked along. "Why did the woolly mammoth cross the road?"

Dakota groaned and rolled his eyes. "I don't suppose it's because he wanted to get to the other side?"

"Of course not," said Shelly using her superior know-it-all tone of voice. "The woolly mammoth crossed the road because there weren't any chickens in the ice age!"

Shelly, PaleoJoe, and Dimitri laughed. Sadie jumped on her hind legs and yipped happily in what Dakota thought sounded suspiciously like doggie laughter.

"Thanks a lot," he told her. "I don't suppose that anyone cares that there weren't any roads in the ice age either?"

Apparently no one did.

"Hey, PaleoJoe," said Shelly. "What do you call Dakota under the foot of a woolly mammoth?"

PaleoJoe grinned and scratched his beard. "I give up," he said.

"Flat!" Shelly giggled.

"Oh ha, ha," said Dakota.

They were approaching the hill now and Dakota jogged ahead. "Race you to the top," he shouted to Shelly.

"That's not fair," she squealed as she took off after him. "You have a head start."

But the head start didn't do Dakota any good.

As he reached the halfway point up the hill, he stubbed his toe on something sticking out of the frozen ground, lost his balance, and went tumbling, head over big toe, back down to the bottom of the hill.

"Ouch," he said, rolling to his feet and rubbing his elbow where he had banged it on the ground.

"Is anything broken?" asked PaleoJoe, helping him to his feet.

Dakota made a face as he watched Shelly make it to the top of the hill and pump her fists in the air in victory.

"That's so not fair," he grumbled.

"What happened?" asked PaleoJoe.

"I'm all right," said Dakota. "The hill tripped me. That's all."

"Hey PaleoJoe!" Shelly's screech was loud enough to be heard on the other side of the Arctic Circle. "Look what Dakota tripped on!"

Dakota, PaleoJoe, Dimitri, and Sadie scrambled up the hill to Shelly. She was kneeling next to something that protruded from the ground. She had taken out her tool roll and was carefully brushing away frozen ground.

"Look," she said. "What is it, PaleoJoe?"

PaleoJoe only needed one quick look to see exactly what it was. "It's a mammoth tooth," he said.

129

CHAPTER TWENTY-FOUR

INTRUDER IN CAMP

"It's huge," said Shelly.

"No wonder I tripped," said Dakota.

"Be honest," said Shelly. "You tripped because you are clumsy. It is just luck that you were clumsy over a cool fossil."

"Luck is my middle name," said Dakota.

"Bad luck," Shelly giggled.

"Okay you two," PaleoJoe intervened. "I think you should help each other now and dig up that fossil. It looks like a good one, Shelly. Dimitri and I will have a look around for caverns."

"Or blue tusks," said Dimitri, smiling through his tangle of beard.

"Take Sadie," said Shelly. But it was obvious

that Sadie, unlike most normal dogs, was not interested in digging up bones. She was dancing on ahead eager to explore over the crest of the hill.

"Crazy dog," laughed Dakota.

While Shelly and Dakota worked together to free the mammoth tooth from the frozen ground, Dimitri, and PaleoJoe, along with Sadie, scouted the area for a likely hiding place for the Blue Tusks.

Poking under the overhang of a shallow cavern PaleoJoe reflected that it was like looking for the needle in a haystack. But all they could do was look. He knew that entombed in the permafrost of this peninsula were the remains of thousands of ice age animals. It was a trove of fossils. And all he wanted to find was one particular, unique fossil among them all.

"Find anything, Dimitri?" he called to the other man who had appeared on the far side of the hill.

"No," Dimitri shouted back.

"Let's get back to camp." He motioned with his arm and went to find Shelly and Dakota.

Covered with smears of dirt, Shelly and Dakota had been successful in digging out the mammoth tooth.

"Look at this, PaleoJoe," said Shelly holding the giant tooth in her hands. It was about the size of a lunchbox and it was heavy.

"It's a molar," said PaleoJoe. "We'll take it back to camp to examine it."

Shelly and Dakota took turns carrying the

131

mammoth molar. Dakota was happy to see the camp come into sight at last. He was just about to say something to that effect when Sadie suddenly started barking in loud, rapid *yips*. Kicking up small spurts of frosted snow, the little dog raced for the camp.

"Sadie!" yelled Dakota. "Where are you going?"

"Look," pointed PaleoJoe. "Someone is trying to raid our camp!"

Quickly Shelly whipped out her binoculars and focused in on the cluster of tents and equipment. Sure enough, there was an intruder.

"It's an arctic fox," she said excitedly. "Look, Dakota!" She handed him the binoculars. Dakota, having trouble adjusting them, was in time to see a suddenly, very fierce, black poodle in close pursuit of a frantically scurrying white fox. Dakota watched as the black blotch chased the ghost-white blotch for several yards away from the camp. Sadie skittered to a stop, sending a series of sharp barks after the fleeing fox.

Shelly cheered.

"I bet he won't be back anytime soon," laughed Dimitri.

Sadie pranced back to meet her humans and to tell them not to worry. She had taken care of everything.

"You're a good and brave dog," Shelly told her. Sadie yipped happily. She seemed to agree.

"Okay," said PaleoJoe. "Let's get something to eat and then we can take a look at the molar and the map. We need to make a plan for tomorrow."

CHAPTER TWENTY-FIVE

Much About Molars

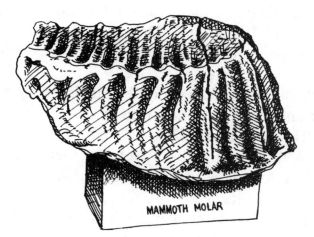

MAMMOTH MOLAR

After supper everyone gathered in the bigger tent to examine the mammoth molar.

Dakota hefted the large tooth in his hand. "I guess they don't call them mammoths for no reason," he said.

"A mammoth's molar had to be big," said Dimitri, "so that he could chew up the large quantities of grass he needed to eat."

"The other interesting thing about mammoth molars," said PaleoJoe examining the fossil Dakota held, "is that mammoths had six sets of teeth in a lifetime."

"Hey Shelly," said Dakota. "What did the tooth fairy say after visiting the baby mammoth?"

Shelly rolled her eyes. "I haven't a clue, but I'm sure you're going to tell me."

"It's a *tusk* job but somebody has to do it," Dakota laughed and then realized that he was the only one. "What? It's funny!" Dakota protested.

"Molars are not tusks, Dakota," Shelly informed him.

"Pish," said PaleoJoe. "Actually ivory is only dentine and is not different from teeth at all."

"Ha!" exclaimed Dakota.

"A mammoth's tusks were its incisors," added Dimitri. "I think that your pun works, Dakota." And he smiled to prove it.

But after so much time had passed since the punch line Dakota did not feel better.

"So if every mammoth lost six sets of teeth in their lifetime, there must be a lot of molars lying around out there," said Shelly. "That's bad news for Dakota. He won't be able to walk anywhere without tripping and falling on his face."

Dakota ignored her.

"It worked like a conveyor belt," said PaleoJoe. "As one set of teeth began to wear down, a new set would erupt from behind them."

"When a mammoth wore out his final set of teeth," said Dimitri, "he starved to death."

"Peachy," said Dakota.

PaleoJoe gently ran his hand over the surface of the molar. "See these marks?" He indicated the grooves in the surface of the molar. Dakota thought they looked a little like shoe treads. "These were ridges of enamel and they were on both the lower and upper teeth. As the animal moved its jaw back and forth, these ridges cut over each other grinding the tough grasses the mammoth ate."

"What about the tusks then?" asked Dakota.

"Mammoths had two sets of tusks in their lifetime," said PaleoJoe. "A smaller set called milk tusks, which were later replaced by the permanent tusks."

"Both males and females had tusks," said Shelly. "They were a very equal species."

"Sure," said Dakota. "But only a male mammoth could make a tusk down! Get it? Touch down—tusk down?"

Shelly gave Dakota a great look of pity. "No one gets that, Dakota," she said.

Dakota sighed. She was probably right.

"The tusks grew like a series of cones stacked

135

together," PaleoJoe continued as though no interruption had taken place. "If you look at a tusk you can see the rings of growth, just like on a tree. You can tell a lot about age and health by studying them."

"How big did the tusks get?" asked Dakota.

"The world record for a woolly mammoth tusk is thirteen and a half feet," said PaleoJoe.

"How long are the Blue Tusks supposed to be?" asked Dimitri suddenly.

There was an uncomfortable silence because no one wanted to give out any more information on the Blue Tusks. Dakota did not actually trust Dimitri yet, and obviously the others were feeling a similar hesitation.

"We don't really know for sure," PaleoJoe answered at last. "We'll need to find them first."

"If you ever do," said Dimitri with a dark stare at Dakota.

And shortly after that Shelly and Dakota returned to their tent. As he was falling asleep, Dakota could hear the sigh of the arctic wind in the big empty land outside. Even bundled in his warm sleeping bag with Sadie curled on his feet, he felt a chill of fear slither down his back.

CHAPTER TWENTY-SIX

SADIE'S WARNING

"It's like looking for that needle in a haystack, PaleoJoe," said Shelly the next day. They had been searching for hours and there had been no sign of the Blue Tusks.

"Pish," said PaleoJoe, even though that had been exactly what he had been thinking.

It had taken them over two hours that morning just to hike to the next cluster of hills. At first, as the treeless hills came into sight, it looked like a promising location. There was even a little lake hiding on the far side. It looked exactly like the sort of spot you would find a cavern or hidden structure of some sort.

But there was nothing.

"Not even a bone hut," said Dakota in disgust. He plopped down on the hard ground. Sadie flopped next to him. They had hiked around the entire base of the hill cluster.

"A little way to the north is a small river," said Dimitri. "I don't know if there are any more likely hills in that direction. Should we take a look?"

"How long will it take to hike there?" asked PaleoJoe.

"Probably a couple of hours," said Dimitri.

PaleoJoe shook his head.

"What are you thinking, PaleoJoe?" asked Shelly.

"Something doesn't feel right about this," said PaleoJoe. "I'm sorry you two, but I don't think we are going to find those Tusks on this trip."

"Ah well," said Dimitri cheerfully. "At least you got to see the tundra and the beautiful land."

"Let's head back to the camp," said PaleoJoe.

Discouraged, they began the long trek back. Dakota, thinking about how he might use his converted skateboard on the hills closer to camp, was the first to notice Sadie's odd behavior. The little poodle had begun a nervous pacing out away from the group and then back again. And now she started up a fretful whine.

"PaleoJoe, there's something wrong with Sadie," said Dakota.

PaleoJoe watched the dog for a minute with a frown on his face. "She's probably cold," he said. "Why don't you carry her for a bit, Dakota?"

Dakota scooped up Sadie and zipped her into the front of his jacket so just her head poked out. The dog didn't protest, but she also didn't stop her fretful whine.

When they got back to camp PaleoJoe said he was going to contact Aunt Felicia to make sure the helicopter would pick them up in the morning.

"There is no reason to stick around," he said.

Dakota agreed with him. But as Dakota ducked back into his tent to wait for PaleoJoe to finish the phone call, he felt a strange sense of uneasiness. Sadie would not stop her fretful whine. And even though the sun was shining there seemed to be a strange, quiet heaviness in the air. *It's just my imagination,* Dakota thought. Still, he felt uneasy.

And then PaleoJoe started to shout. Dakota tumbled from the tent. Shelly and Dimitri were already gathered around PaleoJoe.

"What is it?" asked Dakota.

"A storm," said PaleoJoe his voice tense. "Now don't worry. We should be okay. But we need to secure the tents. The helicopter can't get to us until this storm blows over, so we need to make sure we are prepared to withstand the wind and cold of this little storm."

"How little?" asked Dimitri.

But PaleoJoe didn't answer. He just looked concerned and that made Dakota very uneasy. Concern for PaleoJoe was fear for anyone else.

CHAPTER TWENTY-SEVEN

ATTACK OF THE ARCTIC STORM

The storm hit later that night and it was a monster. The wind howled with furious thunder. Shelly couldn't block it out even by burying her head in her sleeping bag. The roar made it terribly hard to think and Shelly needed to think or she would be scared.

Both tents rocked and flapped as though caught in the talons of a huge monster. *This is what it would be like to be attacked by a T-Rex,* thought Shelly. But as a thought meant for distraction, this wasn't one of her better ones.

Dakota and Shelly and Sadie huddled in their smaller tent. They couldn't even talk to each other over the noise of the battered tent and the blizzard.

Dakota was trying to devise some sort of hand signal language, mostly to keep his mind off the jerking, shuddering tent. He had just figured out a clever way to indicate a desire for a vacation in the tropics when suddenly the door flap to their tent was violently ripped open. A gust of bone chilling wind roared in along with two figures that looked like abominable snowmen.

"PaleoJoe!" Shelly shrieked.

Sadie, who had tried to warn her humans about this terrible storm, cowered further into Dakota's sleeping bag with just her black whiskered nose visible. Dakota dived for the tent flap and struggled to close it against the monster strength of the blizzard trying to engulf them all.

PaleoJoe and Dimitri lay gasping on the floor. Both men had ice crystals in their beards and hair. They looked like the frozen fish stacked in the ice tunnel at Khatanga.

"Our tent blew away," PaleoJoe gasped. "We barely made it."

Quickly Shelly and Dakota piled extra clothing and blankets on the two shivering men. In the small confines of a tent built for three, everybody was pretty much crammed together anyway. *Think warm thoughts,* thought Dakota furiously.

Outside the wind continued to howl. The tent shuttered and rocked back and forth. Dakota wondered what was actually holding it together.

Then there was an awful ripping sound. Apparently nothing was holding it together. Their tent was ripping apart. PaleoJoe lunged for the wildly flapping piece of nylon canvas. He tried to hold it closed but the wind tore it from his grasp, and a bone-chilling cold flooded the tent once again.

There was another awful ripping noise. A new tear appeared in the opposite corner.

"What are we going to do?" Shelly screamed above the roar of the storm.

Wide-eyed, Dakota watched as the tent suddenly began to bulge around the zippered door flap, as though a bear was attacking it. Did polar bears attack helpless scientists in the middle of arctic blizzards? Dakota wondered about this as panic tap-danced in his chest.

Then the flap ripped open and a large hairy face frosted with ice crystals poked in. It wasn't a bear though because it spoke.

"Ah, there are people in here," the hairy face yelled. "Thought so. Better come with me now. Your tent won't last much longer."

Thinking quickly, Dakota bundled together his sleeping bag holding Sadie. A large mittened hand was extended to Dakota. Dakota grasped it and clutching Sadie tightly, hoping the little dog wouldn't suffocate, allowed himself to be pulled from the tent after the others and into the raging blizzard.

The sharp ice crystals, driven by the violent wind, stung his exposed face. Using one hand Dakota cinched his hood down as best he could. This cut out most of the razor sharp snow, but it also limited his vision.

But not before he had seen a very strange sight.

Maybe I'm dreaming, he thought.

All around him in the howling, berserk chaos of the storm, Dakota could see the ghostly shapes of animals that resembled elk. The stocky bodies and magnificent antlers of the snow-covered creatures told Dakota exactly what they were.

Reindeer.

CHAPTER TWENTY-EIGHT

A REINDEER RESCUE

Half blinded by the white sheets of icy snow, and mostly frozen by the unbelievable cold, Dakota waited while their rescuer helped everyone out from the ruined tent.

"This way!" the man bellowed, waving for everyone to follow him.

Dakota felt as though he were fighting a hurricane as they pushed and jostled their way through the roar of the blizzard. All around them the reindeer, packed tightly together, were like ghostly statues. And then suddenly, through the whirl of dark and snow, Dakota caught a glimpse of something that looked like a large white cube.

Their rescuer staggered toward the cube and then

turning, he grabbed Dakota and Shelly shoving them at the strange structure.

"Inside," he shouted.

A door in the side of the cube popped open. Dakota and Shelly found themselves pushed inside. The door slammed closed behind them cutting off the thundering roar of the blizzard. They were no longer being buffeted by the chilling wind.

Dakota stood blinking in the sudden calm. Beside him Shelly, looking like a pink snowman, blinked back at him. There seemed to be several people all bustling about inside the cramped interior. A babble of voices surrounded them.

Dakota unfolded the sleeping bag allowing an impatiently squirming Sadie to escape. The little dog leaped to the floor. She began dancing merrily with happy sharp barks around the shins of a little boy.

"Sadie!" the boy exclaimed, scooping the little poodle into his arms and allowing his face to be licked. Dakota thought the boy was probably only a little older than Miles.

"Welcome," a soft voice greeted them.

Shelly pushed back her hood and found herself looking at a girl dressed in a reindeer skin jacket. Long black braids rested over her shoulders and she had friendly dimples in her round cheeks. Shelly thought the girl was just a little younger than herself.

"My name is Alia," said the girl. "And you are welcome in our *balok*."

145

"Hi," Shelly smiled back. "I'm Shelly and this is Dakota. Thanks for rescuing us."

"You are welcome," said Alia. "It was the reindeer who knew you were there. Later you may say thank you to them."

Dakota looked around the interior of the small room. "What did you call this place?" he asked.

"*Balok*," said Alia in her soft voice. "We are the Dolgan. The *balok* are our homes."

It was about the size of small garage, he thought. It was crowded with people, a table, a stove, and several chairs. Besides Alia and the boy there was an elderly woman leaning with her elbows on the red checked cloth of the table. She grinned at them from a round and wrinkled face. A man was stoking a fire in the stove and a woman was hurrying around Shelly and Dakota trying to help them discard their wet outer jackets.

"My aunt has told me about the Dolgans," said Shelly, squirming out of her snowy jacket. "You are nomadic reindeer herders."

Alia nodded her head. "Please sit down," she said indicating chairs at the table. "This is my Grandmother. That is my father, my mother and my brother, Marko."

Marko set Sadie down and gave a small nod as he was introduced.

"Sadie seems to know you," said Dakota.

Marko grinned and nodded and then dug into his pocket bringing out a fistful of marbles. With a wide grin on his face he held them out to Dakota.

"They do not speak any English," said Alia. "Sadie comes with Uncle Bruno to visit. Uncle Bruno gave Marko the marbles. He wants to show them to you. Do you know Russian?"

"No, I'm afraid not," said Shelly. Dakota shook his head.

"That's okay," Alia smiled. "Uncle Bruno taught me how to speak English and I like the practice." She said something in Russian to Marko who scowled and put the marbles back into his pocket. Dakota gave him a wink to let him know that they could look at the marbles a little later. *When my hands and toes have thawed out,"* thought Dakota.

Marko grinned back and chased Sadie under the table. Alia's father finished stoking the fire and sat down at the table next to Alia's grandmother. He called out something in Russian and smacked the table with his hand making the grandmother jump. She shook her finger at him but didn't look too displeased.

Alia's mother said something that sounded cheerful. Shelly didn't understand a word of it. But a minute later when Alia's mother set steaming cups of milk down in front of everybody, she realized it didn't matter.

"Reindeer milk," said Alia. "But wait, before you drink there is one more thing you need." She jumped up from the table and rummaged inside a large cupboard finally bringing out a candy bar. Breaking off a small square of the chocolate she dropped a piece in Dakota's

147

mug. A little drop of steamy milk plopped out of the mug onto Dakota's hand.

"Ow," he said absently watching the dark chocolate of the piece of candy begin to swirl in the milk.

"Big baby," said Shelly as Alia dropped a piece of chocolate in her mug. "Too cold—too hot. You're never happy."

"Wait just a moment for it to melt," said Alia. "Then drink."

Dakota, ignoring Shelly, waited as long as he could and then scalded his tongue on the hot drink. But as the warm chocolaty flavor filled his mouth, it made him feel almost toasty.

Alia smiled and her father smacked the table again with his hand. He raised his mug in the air. Everybody followed his example. He said something in Russian and then everybody drank. It was a toast of some sort, Dakota decided. Not that he cared right at that moment. It was enough to get hot drink inside him.

"It is very good," Shelly said.

"You might need a spoon to stir it up a little," said Alia. "Here is one." Alia reached across the table for a spoon that rested in the middle of the table. As she did, the sleeve of her jacket pulled back to reveal her wrist.

"Oh!" exclaimed Shelly. "Dakota, look!"

Encircling Alia's wrist was a delicate silver bracelet. And dangling from the silver chain was a blue pendant in the shape of a reindeer head.

Dakota, looking up from his hot chocolate, saw immediately that the small charm looked exactly like the odontolite necklace.

CHAPTER TWENTY-NINE

MAMMOTH HUNTER

"Alia," said Shelly excitedly. "Could I see your bracelet?"

As Alia snatched up the spoon she slid her sleeve back down hiding the bracelet. "Here is your spoon," she said to Shelly as though she had not heard Shelly's request.

Shelly exchanged a puzzled look with Dakota. "Alia," she tried again. "That's a pretty bracelet you are wearing. Could I take a look at it?"

Alia frowned and looked down at the table. *She doesn't want to show it to me,* thought Shelly in sudden understanding. But that was strange too. Why not?

Just then, from where she crouched under the table with Marko, Sadie set up a frenzied burst of sharp barks.

Startled, Dakota dumped a little of his milk on the back of his hand. "Hopping *Iguanodons*, dog," he said. "What is the matter with you?"

But even as he was saying this the door burst open and the man that had rescued them burst into the room. Blizzard and cold swirled in setting Alia's grandmother to scolding and her father to banging on the table again.

The man's sudden entrance caused a lot of excitement. Marko scooted up and over the table as Sadie scooted from under the table. The man was attacked on both fronts with an excited babble of Russian from Marko, and a blast of barking from Sadie.

The man laughed. "Hold to, you wild frooks," he bellowed. "Let a man thaw out, can't you?"

This was followed by another spatter of Russian on all sides. Marko had his fistful of marbles out waving them in the air. Sadie danced on her hind feet and barked. Alia had also rushed forward and was hugging the giant man, snow and all, while her mother started preparing another mug of hot milk.

Dakota and Shelly sat open mouthed at the ruckus and didn't know quite what to do.

The man took off his outer coat shaking snow all over Marko and Sadie. "Greetings Shelly and Dakota," he said over the commotion swirling around him. "Allow me to introduce myself over this wild freckle. I am Bruno Kincaid, Mammoth

Hunter. At your service."

"We know who you are," said Shelly excitedly. "My great aunt named a woolly rhino after you!"

"Yes she did," said Bruno. A squinched look came over his face as though he were experiencing pain. "Your great aunt is a great woman, but she does have her mad hares to chase."

"In other words," said Shelly wisely, "you would rather not have a woolly rhino named after you."

"That is it in the shell of a nut," Bruno agreed. "After all, I am a Mammoth Hunter." He banged his chest with his fist. "Now those are the woolly creatures after one would wish to be acknowledged. Besides, it was Sadie here who found the rhino beastie, not I."

Sadie gave a happy bark when she heard her name.

"Where is PaleoJoe?" asked Shelly.

"PaleoJoe and that fellow that looks like a squinty eyed rabbit are warm and safe in the *balok* next door. I've put you here with my young friends because these homes are very small. I hope that is okay with you."

"Thank you," said Shelly.

"We appreciate the rescue," added Dakota.

"Are you cold, Laddie?" asked the man. "You're shaking like a loose leaf on the wind."

"Dakota is always cold," said Shelly.

"I'm fine," said Dakota, but the truth was when the wind blasted into the small cabin of the *balok*, it had gone straight through Dakota and he was shivering again.

152

The man said something in Russian to Alia's mother. The woman gave Dakota a worried look out of her friendly round face and hurriedly provided him with another cup of hot milk. She also wrapped a large blanket around him leaving only his nose poking out from the hooded cowl of it and his hands relatively free to handle his mug of milk.

"It's an improvement," said Shelly grinning. "You are almost entirely invisible."

"When I stop shaking I'll laugh," grumbled Dakota.

As Dakota was allowing himself to be bundled up like a refugee mummy, Alia had slipped over to Bruno and was whispering something in his ear.

"Ah. I see," said Bruno. "It's okay, Alia. Shelly and Dakota know. You can show them."

"Show us what?" asked Shelly.

Everybody had settled down around the table once more. Sadie had retreated underneath where she took up residence on Dakota's warmly blanketed feet. Marko, on the floor, got out his marbles and began rolling them around.

"Uncle Bruno gave it to me to keep safe," said Alia softly. "I didn't know what to do when you noticed it."

She pulled back the sleeve of her coat. The slender silver bracelet with the little blue pendant dangled from her wrist. Alia held it out for Shelly to look at. "Go ahead," said Alia. "You may unhook it."

The piece of jewelry slipped into her hand as Shelly released the clasp.

"I wish I had PaleoJoe's loupe," said Shelly squinting at the pendant as she held it close to her eyes.

"No need for any confabulated twaddle," said Bruno Kincaid. "I can tell you what you are wondering about. That reindeer is like the reindeer carving you have, Miss Brooks. And yes, it is a map."

Dakota, the shivering now subsiding into the occasional shudder, was thinking hard. "Is it the same map as the one carved on the pendant we have?" he asked.

"No," said Bruno looking darkly at Dakota. "It is different."

"Is it a map to the Blue Tusks?" asked Shelly.

"Shelly!" said Dakota sharply.

"I think he knows all about it already," said Shelly irritably.

"Indeed I do," said Bruno. "But your young friend is right to be cautious, Lassie. For hundreds of years many people have hunted for the Blue Tusks and not all who seek it are honest."

"Well, you must be honest or Aunt Felicia would not have named her woolly rhino after you," said Shelly defending herself.

"Wait a minute," said Dakota thinking it through. "That can't be the map to the Blue Tusks. If it were, then you would have already found them."

"True," said Bruno.

"I don't get it," said Shelly. "Why would there be two maps?"

"There isn't," said Dakota, feeling a shiver of excitement adding itself to his shiver of cold. "It's all one map, isn't it Mr. Kincaid?" Dakota was feeling very excited now. He knew he understood it at last.

"Shelly," he said. "Don't you get it? The reason we couldn't find where the Blue Tusks are hidden is because we had only half of a map. You need both reindeer carvings to have all of the map. Right?" he demanded looking at Bruno Kincaid. "Am I right?"

"Yes," said the Mammoth Hunter. "Dakota Jackson, you are right. And in the morning, we are going to find them."

CHAPTER THIRTY

A PLACE TO START

"Look here," said Bruno Kincaid.

Out of his pocket he pulled the map that Mr. Zephaniah had drawn from the carving on the first pendant. From another pocket Bruno took out another piece of paper with another map drawn on it.

"This is from Alia's pendant," he said. "Now the scale of the two maps do not match, of course, but look here." He traced a large blunt finger along a line on the first map. "This is where you were looking. See these cross hatch marks on your map?"

"We thought they marked the spot where the tusks were hidden," said Dakota.

"What they mark," said Bruno, "is the place where the two maps should be joined together. See?"

He placed the maps in position. The two maps were drawn in different scale sizes, but it was easy to see how the second map was a continuation of the first.

"Now, see how the line continues on this map?" His finger jumped over to the second map to trace a line there.

"Yes," said Shelly thoughtfully. "It is a continuation. And look. There is a mark on your map that is unmistakable." She pointed to the tracing of the outline of a reindeer.

"I agree with you, Lassie," said Bruno. "I put that mark there to indicate just that. Let me explain.

"On Alia's carving there is a mark that looks like the eye of a reindeer. And notice that on the pendant itself the reindeer's eye is a hole."

"My pendant isn't like that," said Shelly.

Bruno smiled. "That's good because it's my theory that only one carving can tell the actual location. I placed Alia's carving on the map and aligned the hole with the eye."

"I get it," said Dakota. "By lining them up like that the branches of the antlers on the carving indicated where the Blue Tusks might be hidden."

"Exactly so," said Bruno. "But I did not know how to find that place without knowing where I should start. Your map tells me that."

"Will this storm be over tomorrow?" asked Dakota from the cave of his blanket. "Will we be able to go and look?"

157

"Yes and yes," said Bruno. "But now I think we should all go to bed so we can be rested."

"Tell us about the mammoths first," said Alia. "Uncle Bruno, if we are going to search for them tomorrow, you know that the proper thing to do is to tell their story first. That way they will not be angry if you find them."

"Exactly correct," Bruno nodded his head.

"What does that mean?" asked Dakota.

"The Dolgans do not like to disturb the bones that lie hidden in the ground," explained Bruno. "It's okay for them to pick up the bones that make their way to the surface but they believe that digging up the bones will bring bad luck and even death."

Dakota gulped. He didn't like curses or superstition.

"Nonsense," said Shelly impatiently. She was a scientist and did not believe in superstition. "That's just superstition."

"That might be," said Bruno. "But it is always polite and courteous for a person to be respectful of the beliefs of others, especially when you are a stranger in such a very cold place."

Shelly nodded. "I see your point."

"Tell the story then, Uncle Bruno," Alia demanded.

"Finish your milk," said Bruno nodding his shaggy head. "Then let's get settled."

So they finished their drinks of hot milk. Alia's

158

mother and father and Marko, who was yawning so hard his jaws were cracking, retired to the small adjoining bedroom. Shelly and Dakota helped Alia's grandmother pull out a cot next to the stove. The elderly woman smiled her thanks and patted Dakota's face with a gentle gnarled hand. With Sadie cuddled up under her chin, she wrapped herself up in some blankets and was soon snoring gently.

Bruno, Shelly, Dakota, and Alia gathered around the table once again. Outside the *balok* the blizzard blew with a loud thundering roar. They could hear the wind pounding the sides of the small house. Dakota wrapped himself up in his blanket thinking about the herd of reindeer standing out in the storm. He wondered how they could tolerate such weather.

"Now, listen carefully young people, and I will tell you a story that the galoots of the world have no idea about," said Bruno. "Are you listening? It's important."

Shelly, Dakota, and Alia nodded eagerly. They did not want to be galoots. They were listening.

"Then," said Bruno Kincaid, Mammoth Hunter, "I will begin."

CHAPTER THIRTY-ONE

MYSTERIOUS MAMMOTHS

"I will begin 11,ooo years ago," Bruno Kincaid began his story.

His voice was a low rumble in the quiet *balok*. "The native people living across Siberia thought the bones of mammoths belonged to a race of giant rats that lived underground. When a giant rat accidentally came up into the sunshine it was instantly killed. That's why there were so many bones about, you see."

"Galoots," commented Dakota.

"Without a doubt," nodded Bruno. "But today the biggest mystery about the mammoths is what happened to them. There are three theories."

"Good," said Shelly. "I like theories."

"I like beef jerky," said Dakota. "Wish I had

some right now."

Shelly gave him a look. Alia giggled.

"Theory number one," said Bruno holding up his thumb, "is the Overchill Theory."

"That's what Dakota suffers from," said Shelly.

Dakota tried to kick her under the table but his feet were bundled up in the large blanket so the effort was wasted.

"According the Overchill Theory," Bruno continued, "the mammoth died because the advance of the polar sheets killed off the vegetation they were eating. Plant life became the less nutritional glop of mosses and sedges."

"Glop?" Dakota raised his eyebrows.

"A highly scientific term meaning whatever the scientist using it means it to mean," said Bruno scowling.

"Sorry," Dakota quickly apologized.

"The problem with the Overchill Theory is that in North America there is no evidence that the mammoth were suffering from malnutrition at the end of the Pleistocene. And other fossils that have been found suggest that the mammoth were dying out long before the end of the Great Ice Age."

"So much for theory #1," said Shelly. "What's theory #2?"

Bruno winked at her. "Theory #2 is called the OverKill Theory," he said. "Early hunters spreading across the continent brought with them a new skill.

They knew how to chip spear points from flint. These points were very distinctive. They were two to three inches long and leaf shaped with a wide groove. The first one was discovered in 1952. The people who made them are named after a rich trove of the spear points found in Clovis, New Mexico. They are called Clovis Hunters."

"Did the Clovis Hunters kill the mammoth? Is that the theory?" asked Shelly.

"Scientists ask that very question, Lassie. Did the Clovis Hunters hunt to extinction the biggest game ever?" Bruno jabbed the tabletop with his finger for emphasis. "The Clovis Hunters were armed with their flint spear points and they had also developed a tool called an *atlatl*. It was a stick that could sling a spear at high speeds."

"I sense a problem with this theory," said Dakota, watching Bruno's face.

"You are correct, Laddie. There is indeed a great hitch in this theory. It turns out that there is no real physical evidence to support it. Clovis points are very common to find across the North American continent, but there have only been fifteen locations where the Clovis points have been found alongside of mammoth bones that appear to be scraped or gouged by humans."

"That sort of complicates that theory, then," said Shelly.

"Oh yes," said Bruno. "And not only that, but

nowhere has anyone found evidence to suggest that the Clovis Hunters hunted any of the other big animals that also became extinct around the same time as the mammoths. The giant ground sloths, camels, and woolly rhinos also disappeared."

"Is there a theory #3?" asked Dakota.

"Of course," Bruno smiled and tapped the side of his nose. "Scientists are always thinking. Theory #3 is called the Hyperdisease Theory. Recently some scientists have proposed the idea that perhaps the Clovis Hunters or maybe their dogs, introduced a super bug, like a virus, that devastated the mammoths.

"There are many examples of such super bugs causing terrible damage to animal and human populations, too. For example, in 1990 there was a fungus that somehow slipped into the population of the golden toad in Costa Rica. Since 1995, no one has seen a golden toad anywhere."

"Gosh," said Dakota. "That doesn't sound good."

"It isn't," Bruno agreed. "In fact, it's very bad. A deadly microbe or a killer plague could very well have been responsible for the extinction of the woolly mammoths. There has been no evidence found to support this theory yet, but it is a new theory and so we have only just begun to look.

"And so now you know about these mysterious beasties whose tusks we will seek in the morning. If we find the Blue Tusks, we will have solved one mystery

163

at least. Now we must get some sleep."

Quietly, so not to disturb Alia's grandmother, Dakota and Bruno folded away the kitchen table. Shelly helped Alia drag out blankets and pillows and everyone found a place on the floor.

Shelly was squeezed in between Alia and the cold wall of the *balok*. Outside the sounds of the blizzard seemed to be diminishing. She sighed, closed her eyes, and almost immediately drifted into sleep.

Dakota found himself wedged between Bruno and Alia but decided it was okay because it was warmest to be squished in the middle. And it really wasn't until Bruno, sounding like a herd of mammoth on the march, started to snore that anyone had any trouble with sleeping.

CHAPTER THIRTY-TWO

THE HUNT

The next morning the blizzard had blown itself out.

"Wake up, Shelly!" Alia's soft voice brought Shelly out of a sound sleep.

Sitting up and rubbing her eyes, Shelly groggily saw that she and Alia were the only ones in the balok.

"Where is everyone?" she asked.

"Outside," said Alia. "The storm is gone and everyone is getting ready to go find the Blue Tusks. We are going to take the *baloks* part of the way. We are following the wild reindeer herds and they have moved in the same direction that you want to go. But then you will have to take dogsleds the rest of the way. Come on!"

Shelly did not have to be urged any more. Together the two girls folded up the blankets and cleared the space on the floor. They set the kitchen table back up just as Alia's mother opened the door and came in. She was carrying a pail of milk. She held it up with a smile.

"Mother will have breakfast ready soon," said Alia. "Reindeer meat and scrambled eggs. Eggs are very scarce, but Uncle Bruno brought us some."

"I need to find PaleoJoe," said Shelly.

"I will show you," said Alia. "Follow."

The two girls stepped outside of the balok into the bright morning sunlight and sudden chaos.

"Sheeeelllllllleeeeeee! Look at meeeeeeeee!"

It was, of course, Dakota.

"What are you doing?" Shelly screeched as Dakota, in a highly unusual maneuver, swished past in a swirl of snow.

Dakota, fastened somehow to his converted skateboard, was being pulled along behind a reindeer. Grasping the reins fastened to the animal with both hands, Dakota was shouting to Marko who ran alongside him carrying a long pole-like stick.

"Oh no," gasped Alia. "That's a reindeer accelerator."

"What is that?" asked Shelly.

"Now!" shouted Dakota to Marko.

Marko lowered the pole into position and poked the reindeer in a strategic spot. The result was very dramatic.

The reindeer tucked its tail and put on a marvelous burst of speed.

"Yahoooo!" yelled Dakota, skimming along behind the animal as though he were waterskiing and being pulled by a powerboat.

And it all worked fine until the reindeer took a sharp turn to the right and Dakota went on sailing to the left. The reins jerked out of his hand and for one brief moment he was slightly airborne as he hit an icy hump of snow. Then he came crashing down in a spectacular explosion of snow, skateboard and boy.

"Dakota, are you all right?" Shelly and Alia ran to help him.

"I'm—mooof—perfectly—umpf—fine." Dakota snorted snow out of his nose.

"And now," said PaleoJoe who had watched the whole escapade and was not finding it amusing, "if you are quite through messing around, we have an expedition to start." And then he sneezed. "Before I die of pneumonia," he added.

The reindeer were hitched to the *baloks*, and with a lot of calling and shouting back and forth among the Dolgan, they started out. The *baloks* were truly remarkable. The small cabins were constructed on skid cradles. Teams of reindeer were harnessed to each house, and the *baloks* were pulled across the tundra at a very good speed.

Reindeer snorted white clouds of breath, the

167

harnesses jingled, dogs barked, children called and laughed to each other, and the whole community was suddenly on the move.

Around mid-day, Alia and Marko said a temporary good-bye to Shelly and Dakota. Bruno had hitched up three dogsleds. Shelly rode with PaleoJoe, and Dakota and Sadie went with Bruno. Dimitri carried most of the supplies on his sled.

"We'll meet up with you this evening," called Alia as the reindeer were prodded into motion once again. "Bye!"

Shelly waved at her friend and watched as the reindeer, in a swirl of frozen snow, pulled the white cubed *baloks* over the hill and out of sight.

"Okay," said Bruno. "We need to travel about an hour in that direction. Let's move!"

The sleds, pulled by teams of huskies, sliced through the new snow with a hissing sound. They made good time. Before Dakota even had time to get bored, Bruno was pulling the sled to a stop.

"Okay," he said as everyone gathered around him. "According to the map we should be in the area."

Dakota, wearing the special reflective sunglasses given to him by his friend Cleveland Sanders, squinted across the tundra. There didn't seem to be a lot there. Across the horizon there was a pile of rocks that looked promising but they were in the wrong direction. *That can't be it,* thought Dakota.

"Over there," said PaleoJoe. He pointed in the

direction of a cluster of small hills. It looked just like the cluster of treeless hills that they had investigated earlier.

PaleoJoe felt a moment of discouragement. His nose was red from more than just the cold air. He sniffled and sneezed. He was getting a cold. He could feel it. When his tent had blown away, the sudden dreadful chill had seemed to trigger a reaction in his system. He thought he needed a warm bed and a hot cup of coffee. But that would have to wait. And his cold could just wait, too. First they would find the Blue Tusks.

"Let's break up into teams," he said.

"I'll go with Bruno," Dakota volunteered. He was anxious to see a Mammoth Hunter in action.

"Shelly, you're with me," said PaleoJoe. Only because his nose was stuffed up, it came out as *bee* not *me*.

"Buzz, buzz," smiled Shelly.

"I'll check that far ridge," Dimitri volunteered.

And so they set out.

It took them three hours. Three hours to find nothing.

CHAPTER THIRTY-THREE

WHAT WAS MISSED

"Shelly, I need to talk to you. I think we've missed something," said Dakota. He had been searching all through the Dolgan camp trying to find her. At last he had caught up to her as she was coming out of the balok where PaleoJoe was staying.

"Leave me alone, Dakota," she snapped at him. Shelly was in a bad mood. They had not found the Blue Tusks. PaleoJoe was sick with a bad cold and he had just informed her that they would be leaving tomorrow.

"Another early storm is coming," PaleoJoe had said. Only because of his cold it had sounded like: *Udnuder early storb is cobbig.* "We have to leave."

"But what about the Blue Tusks?" Shelly had asked. "We can't just leave without finding them."

"No one has found them for hundreds of years," said PaleoJoe. He carefully measured out a spoonful of cold medicine. "It's unreasonable to expect that we can just walk in and find them in a couple of hours."

"But we have a map," Shelly pointed out, watching PaleoJoe hold his nose as he took the medicine.

"Maybe we can come back next season and look some more," said PaleoJoe. He curled up on his cot and pulled his blankets over his head closing his eyes. A final sneeze shook the entire bed and blanket mountain that was PaleoJoe.

And that's when Shelly had stomped out of the *balok* only to run into Dakota who, most likely, had some harebrained scheme to ski off the roof of one of the *baloks*.

"Shelly, stop," persisted Dakota following her. "Just listen. I think I know why we didn't find the tusks."

Shelly sighed and stopped walking. "Why?" She put her hands on her hips and frowned at him.

"We were looking in the wrong place," said Dakota.

"Well, obviously," said Shelly. "If we had been looking in the right place I suspect we would have found them."

"No, you don't understand," said Dakota. "Look. Will you just come with me for one minute and let me show you something?"

Shelly sighed and rolled her eyes. "Okay," she

171

said at last. What else was there to do? "Only make it fast."

Shelly followed Dakota back to Alia's *balok*. No one was inside. Everyone was off tending to the reindeer. Dakota brought out Bruno's map.

"Look," he said. "Today we were looking here, in this area." He swirled his finger on the map to show where they had spent several hours looking for the thing they didn't find. "We were looking here because of the trick of the reindeer's eye that Bruno showed us. If you place the carving here, with this mark as its eye, it seems clear that the swirl of the antlers marks where to look for the Blue Tusks."

"Yes," said Shelly feeling more impatient. "What is your point?"

"Can I see your pendant?" asked Dakota.

Another sigh. Shelly grumpily took off the necklace and handed Dakota the carving.

"It's just a theory," said Dakota. "Your carving doesn't have the open circle of the eye in it, but otherwise it's identical in shape and style to Alia's. So this is approximate, but look what happens if we put the carving over the eye mark, only flip down the pendant. Like this." He demonstrated placing the pendant so the scratched surface was face down. "Now the antlers are sweeping in the opposite direction."

Shelly looked thoughtfully at the map. "It's in the same area where we were," she said. "Only now the indication is in the opposite direction." She frowned, thinking. "What was in the opposite direction? Were there more hills?"

"No," said Dakota. "Something better. A ridge of rocks. I thought at the time I saw it that it looked promising, but I didn't say anything because it was off in the opposite direction."

Shelly grabbed Dakota's arm in sudden excitement. "Dakota, I think you might be right."

"I do too," said Dakota. "Let's tell PaleoJoe. Tomorrow we can go back and look." He was out the door before Shelly could stop him.

"Dakota wait!" Shelly scrambled after him. "We can't tell PaleoJoe," she said as she caught up to him.

"Why not?" asked Dakota, stopping in surprise.

"We're leaving tomorrow."

"Then we have to go now," said Dakota. He cinched down his hood and zipped his jacket up to his chin. It was cold.

Shelly shook her head. "PaleoJoe is sick. He's just taken some cold medicine. It's the kind that makes you really sleepy. He would never be able to take us."

"Let's get Bruno then," said Dakota, turning in the other direction.

"Bruno has gone with the herders to bring in the reindeer. He's not around." Shelly's words stopped him again.

Dakota was silent. Frustrated he frowned at Shelly. But as he watched her he saw the fire of determination grow in her eyes. Suddenly he found that his excitement was quickly dying into anxiety.

Uh-oh, he thought. *This is not going to be good.*

"We'll have to go ourselves," said Shelly stating firmly exactly what Dakota was dreading she would say.

"Shelly, we can't," he began the string of arguments that he knew, deep down, would do no good. "We don't know enough about survival on the tundra or even how to drive those dogsleds. It's getting late. It would be dark by the time we started back. We could get lost."

"I watched PaleoJoe drive the sled all day," said Shelly. "He even let me do it for awhile. I can figure it out."

"Figure what out?" It was Dimitri. They had been so involved in their discussion they had not heard him approach.

Shelly and Dakota exchanged a look. Should they trust him? Dimitri might be the only person who could help them. Dakota gave a nod. They would have to risk it.

CHAPTER THIRTY-FOUR

THE BLUE TUSKS

"We'll have to hurry," said Dimitri. "I think we should have just enough time to get there and take a quick look. It might be dark by our return but I think only just. We can do it. You two go ahead and get on the sled. My dogs are still harnessed. I hadn't had time to unhook them yet. I just want to pop back to the *balok* for an extra pair of gloves. I'll tell PaleoJoe where we are going so he won't worry."

"If you can wake him up," said Shelly and Dakota nodded.

"I think this will work out," said Shelly as they waited by the sled.

"Just don't trust him too much," said Dakota uneasily.

175

A rapid high-pitched barking interrupted them as Sadie came bouncing around the corner and jumped aboard. This, of course, set the huskies into a barking, jostling frenzy. Sadie ignored them. Her humans would take care of the riff-raff.

"That dog always knows when adventure is afoot," said Dakota, trying to grab onto the harness of the nearest husky to keep him from getting the traces tangled.

"Okay, let's go," said Dimitri striding up. "PaleoJoe says to be careful and good luck." He grinned and his white teeth flashed in his sinister black beard. "All aboard."

It took an hour to reach the site. Dakota, hungry, found a half frozen packet of Tabasco beef jerky in his pocket. He took out a piece to gnaw on, letting the fiery taste of it burn through his mouth in a simulation of heat. Supper would be late tonight and he was already feeling really hungry. And cold.

They reached the outcroppings of rock and left the dog sled to take a closer look. As they approached they could see that the area was the rocky top of a small hill. During the day the sun had mostly melted the fresh snow that had fallen in the storm the night before, leaving the rocky surface exposed.

It was Sadie who found the cave.

"Over here!" Dakota called to Shelly and Dimitri when he went to investigate the reason for the excited barking of the little dog.

They found Dakota on his stomach, looking into a narrow opening in the surface of the rock.

"I think it's a passage that leads to a cave," said Dakota.

"Let me take a look," said Dimitri. He unclipped a flashlight and got down on his stomach to peer into the dark opening.

"Be careful," Dakota warned him. "There is a lot of loose rock right there. You could cave in the opening pretty easily."

As he said this there was a trickle of rock and a grunt from Dimitri as he almost pitched head first into the hole. Dakota grabbed his belt and heaved him back.

"Thanks," said Dimitri rolling to his feet. "I don't think there is much of a drop. I've got a length of rope on the sled. I could lower one of you down to take a look. I think we should check it out. It looks promising."

"I'll do it," said Dakota.

Dimitri got his rope and tied a length of it around Dakota. Shelly stood to one side watching. She felt a little nervous about this but she didn't really want to go into the dark hole herself.

"Be careful," she said.

Dimitri lowered Dakota into the hole.

"It's not deep at all," Dakota's voice called out almost immediately. And then his hand appeared in the opening waving.

"Dimitri, you could easily climb out," he said. "And you can just give Shelly and me a leg up and we can get out easily too."

"What do you see in there?" asked Shelly.

"It opens up in here. I think there is a cavern just ahead," said Dakota his voice getting fainter as he moved deeper into the cave.

"Dakota wait for us!" Shelly called impatiently.

Sadie scrambled under the overhang and launched herself into the hole after Dakota. Shelly could hear the little dog barking as she followed him.

"Come on," said Dimitri to Shelly. "I'll give you a hand inside."

Dakota could hear Shelly and Dimitri following him as he pushed his way deeper into the cavern. The narrow passageway quickly opened up and Dakota found himself entering a small cave. Frost sparkled on the walls wherever he shone his flashlight. It was absolutely quiet. And very, very cold.

Then, suddenly, the beam of his flashlight bounced off a smooth surface that looked like glass. Quickly Dakota directed his light to that spot and gasped in amazement at what he saw.

He was looking at a wall of ice, only the ice was clear and it was like looking into a glass case at the museum. And inside that case of arctic ice was the treasure they had been seeking.

Two giant tusks were suspended in the glittering ice like ancient animals trapped in a white amber.

Dakota stepped forward shining his light on the length of the ivory and he grinned in astonishment at the vibrant blue of their curved and ancient lengths.

CHAPTER THIRTY-FIVE

AN EXPEDITION INTO DANGER

"Simply amazing," said Dimitri shining his flashlight on the icy wall. He couldn't take his eyes off the Blue Tusks. They were truly the most amazing things he had ever seen.

"How are we going to get them out?" asked Shelly.

"I have a pick-ax in the sled," said Dimitri. "I think we can chop them out. They don't look like they are in there too deep. In any case let's get started. You two wait here and I'll go get the ax."

"How did they get in there?" asked Shelly rubbing her mitten on the glass-like surface. She barely noticed that Dimitri had left them.

"Somehow that Bernard fellow must have figured out a way to encase them in ice," said Dakota. "It's very clever however he did it."

Just then Sadie perked up her ears and then began a deafening barrage of high-pitched barking.

"Sadie!" shouted Shelly covering her ears. "Stop that!"

But the little dog didn't stop. Instead she nipped Dakota on the back of his leg and then raced back for the opening.

"Ow!" yelped Dakota. "She bit me. Sadie you come back here!"

And Dakota started off after the dog.

"Dakota wait for me," said Shelly hurriedly following.

As Dakota reached the opening to the hole he was stunned to see a flurry of rocks and stones pouring into the opening. Sadie was barking in a frenzy, whirling around and jumping up and down.

"Dimitri!" yelled Dakota. "Help us! The hole is caving in!"

But with a sudden sick feeling in the pit of his stomach Dakota realized that Dimitri was not going to help them because it was Dimitri that was caving in the hole.

"Dimitri, stop!" cried Shelly as she too realized what the man was doing.

The rocks and dirt continued to rain in. With a

181

savage growl Sadie leaped at the opening. Her back claws scrabbled against the rocky side of the opening and it looked, for a minute, like she wasn't going to make it. Then she gave great wiggle and heave with her hind legs and she was through.

Shelly and Dakota heard her barking and growling. Then they heard Dimitri yell something angrily. For a brief moment the caving-in stopped. Then there was the sharp yelp of a dog in pain.

Then silence.

The rain of dirt and stones started up again.

"Quick, Shelly," said Dakota. "Let me give you a leg up."

But he was too late. As Shelly put her foot in his cupped hand, a landslide of rock, dirt and ice came crashing in and knocked both of them back. They staggered against the wall, choking on the grit and crystals of ice that filled the small space.

"Shelly, I dropped my flashlight," Dakota cried out in panic.

"I've got mine," Shelly quickly responded and snapped it on.

The sudden yellow glare showed them the cave-in and Dakota almost wished he hadn't looked.

It was bad. The opening to the hole was completely gone. They were sealed in.

"Don't worry," said Shelly, her voice shaking just a little bit. "PaleoJoe will come and look for us when we don't show up."

"Shelly," said Dakota feeling sick to his stomach. "PaleoJoe doesn't know where we are. I don't think Dimitri ever really told him. No one knows where we are."

In the dim light Dakota could see Shelly's shadowy face. He felt as scared as she looked.

CHAPTER THIRTY-SIX

TRAPPED

They decided to return to the cavern where the Blue Tusks were encased in ice. There was a little more room there and they could move around trying to keep warm.

"It must be getting late," said Shelly. "I'm feeling tired."

"We can't go to sleep," said Dakota urgently. "We'll freeze if we do. Here, have some Tabasco beef jerky. That will put some fire in your veins."

Shelly took a strip. They gnawed on the beef jerky feeling the hot spice burn their tongues and throats. It didn't warm them at all.

"Do you think he hurt Sadie?" asked Dakota.

"Yes," said Shelly. She was poking her light into

the corners of the cavern looking for another opening. There didn't seem to be one. "I'm also thinking Dimitri is working in Buzzsaw's gang. There's no proof of course. It's just who else would be such a slimy no good galoot?"

"A real yahoot," Dakota agreed.

"He's trying to murder us, you know," said Shelly in a voice far calmer than the emotion she was feeling.

"I know," said Dakota a sudden flush of anger making him almost warm. "And when I get out of here I'm going to break his arm."

"I'll help," said Shelly.

"Do you think we could dig ourselves out?" asked Dakota.

They decided it was worth a try, but when they returned to the cave-in they discovered that there was far too much dirt and rock. Wherever they tried to dig, more rubble fell down filling in the gap. They gave up and went back to the tusks.

Shelly lay down on the ground.

"I'm so tired," she said. "I'm just going to take a quick little nap. Let me know if anything happens."

"Shelly, no!" Dakota felt real fear twist through his heart. He knew a little bit about hyperthermia from his first aid class. Sleepiness was a bad sign when you were cold. Quickly he bent over Shelly and tried to urge her to her feet. "Get up, Shelly. You can't go to sleep. Walk around a little bit. Come on."

"Leave me alone," Shelly mumbled, slumping

back to the ground.

Dakota looked around in desperation. How could he get Shelly on her feet and moving? And then he had an inspiration.

"Knock-knock," said Dakota.

Shelly opened her eyes and frowned up at him sourly. "I'll pretend I didn't hear that," she said closing her eyes again.

"Come on, Shelly," said Dakota determination sharpening his voice. "KNOCK-KNOCK! You can't ignore me. I won't let you. KNOCK-KNOCK! You have to answer me. You can't leave a knock-knock joke unanswered. That's like not answering the door when someone is there."

Shelly opened her eyes and gave him a very sour look. "Dakota Jackson if you think I'm going to die in a hole playing knock-knock jokes with you—think again!"

"Well right, because you never get them anyway," said Dakota using his most insulting voice.

"Oh, I never get them!" Shelly propped herself up on one elbow and glared at Dakota.

'That's right," said Dakota. "Your mind is too analytical to understand the subtle aspects of the art of knock-knock jokes."

"Well, your brain is so dim you can't understand most of everything else," Shelly sat up now and was ready for full battle.

Dakota smiled grimly to himself. He didn't want

to fight but he knew in order to keep Shelly from falling asleep, he had to do something. His plan was working.

It was then that Shelly's flashlight sputtered and died. Suddenly, in mid-argument they were plunged into complete and total darkness. Shelly gave a little shriek.

"It's okay," she said. "I was just surprised. I'm not afraid of the dark."

"Me either," said Dakota. "I don't, however, like being trapped in the dark in a hole under the frozen tundra of Siberia. It's the prospect of becoming a mummy that worries me."

"Me too," said Shelly in a small voice.

Talking like this, the two found their way to each other. Shelly bumped Dakota's nose with her elbow and they wrapped their arms around each other trying to find some warmth and courage.

"Look," said Dakota after a minute.

"At what?" asked Shelly. "There are so many lovely shades of darkness all around us."

"Over there," Dakota nudged Shelly. She turned her head and let out a small breath of surprise.

"I see it," she said.

The Blue Tusks were glowing in the solid black that surrounded them. Embedded deep in the crystal ice, the long, ancient curved tusks looked like something from the world of magic as they gently glowed a deep and ghostly blue. It wasn't light enough to see by, but it was enough to help them believe that they were not alone in that absolute, frozen darkness.

CHAPTER THIRTY-SEVEN

Rescue

Dakota's head dropped and jerked him awake. How much time had passed? Shelly's head rested heavily on his shoulder. Her weight against him felt limp and lifeless.

"Shelly!" Dakota jostled her in sudden panic. Shelly moaned but she didn't answer him and she remained slumped against him.

How could I be so careless! Dakota thought angrily. He had meant to start up the argument again to keep Shelly alert and awake, but he too had been overcome with tiredness. He still was. It was much too difficult to keep his eyes open…much better to just close them…he felt he could sleep now….

And then suddenly something cannoned into his

stomach and his ears were filled with the shrill sound of a yapping dog. And then his face was being drenched by happy slobber.

"Sadie?" Dakota felt confused. Was he dreaming?

But the little dog was real enough. Now she turned her attention to Shelly who moaned and tried to roll her face away from the insistent reviving slobber of Sadie.

"Mmmfff," said Shelly feebly swatting with her hand.

And now Dakota could hear the sounds of voices and the chink of shovels on dirt. Soon a light appeared and behind it came the burly figure of Bruno Kincaid.

"I've found them!" Bruno shouted over his shoulder. "They are alive!"

And then the small cavern was filled with people. Dakota and Shelly were strapped down onto stretchers and mountains of warm blankets and coverings were wrapped around them. As they were being hoisted out of the cavern, Dakota caught sight of PaleoJoe stroking his beard and peering at the ice wall and the Blue Tusks.

"*Iguanodon* toenails," he said. Only it sounded like *Igwandodon toad-dales* because of his cold. Then there was the flash of a camera and Dakota was hauled out of the cavern, and out of the hole, and up into a very cold and clear arctic night.

As his stretcher was loaded onto a dog sled,

Dakota looked up into the sky where ghostly green and yellow sheets of lights shimmered on the horizon. The Northern Lights. It was the most beautiful thing Dakota had ever seen.

And then he closed his eyes and went into a friendlier darkness.

CHAPTER THIRTY-EIGHT

Shelly Says Thank You

Dakota opened his eyes and through the blur of vanishing sleep discovered he was in the familiar surroundings of Alia's *balok*. A small warm weight on his chest turned out to be a still dozing Sadie. Dakota lay still for a minute more, savoring the warmth of the dog and the blankets. He was as happy as he had ever been to be safe and not trapped in a cave, frozen underground.

He could hear the mummer of voices coming from the small kitchen area. The smell of hot chocolate tickled his nose. Dakota sighed and closed his eyes again.

"Get up, Rip Van Winkle!" The sudden shout was accompanied by something large and fuzzy being

191

dumped on Dakota's face.

"*Mummpff,*" said Dakota, which Sadie correctly interpreted as *What is this thing attacking my face?* The little dog quickly jumped down and headed into the kitchen leaving Dakota to struggle with whatever it was that had attacked them.

Dakota thrashed his way out of his covers and pulled the fuzzy weight off his face. Shelly leaned in the doorway giggling hard enough to make her face as red as her hair.

"Very nice," Dakota snapped. "This is the thanks I get for almost dying with you?"

"It *is* nice, you idiot," smiled Shelly. "Look at it!"

Dakota held up what Shelly had thrown at him. Immediately he could see that the fuzzy weight was a beautifully knitted dark gray sweater. It was soft to the touch and Dakota was sure that the person lucky enough to wear it would be marvelously warm.

"It's made from the hair of musk ox," said Shelly. "They roam all over the tundra, not too far from here. Alia and her mom collect the tufts of hair and then they spin it into yarn, which they use to knit these sweaters. Alia says she'll teach me how."

Dakota put down the sweater and picked up the other item that had been heaped onto his sleeping face. It was a jacket made from reindeer hide. It looked like the one Alia's dad wore, only Dakota could tell it was smaller, more suitable to his own size.

"Are these for me?" he asked.

Shelly nodded, her eyes twinkling. "I traded a few things with Alia for them," she said. Alia was now the proud owner of one pink backpack and a pair of pink tennis shoes. But Shelly felt very happy with her trade.

"Wow," Dakota stroked the soft sweater. He had a feeling that his days of being cold were over. "Thanks," he said feeling a bit shy and grateful all at the same time.

"Mr. Chisholm was quite wrong," said Shelly smugly. "I don't insult the people I like, especially when they try to save my life." And with a toss of her red ponytail she vanished leaving Dakota to blush alone.

Dakota scrambled out of bed and quickly got dressed. He discovered the gray sweater fit him perfectly. It was very warm and he felt good wearing it. When he emerged from the sleeping corner, he found PaleoJoe and Bruno Kincaid sitting at the table waiting for him. Shelly refilled steaming mugs of milk and set one out for Dakota, along with a piece of chocolate. Sadie was chewing on a bone under the table, resting comfortably on Bruno's big foot.

"Alia and her family are out rounding up the reindeer," Shelly told Dakota as he sat down.

"And we have things to discuss," said PaleoJoe blowing his nose in a large blue handkerchief. His cold was better but he was still sniffling.

"How did you find us?" asked Dakota taking a sip of his steamy milk.

"Sadie, of course," said Bruno. "The brave little thing limped back to us and found Alia who came and got me. I chased PaleoJoe out of his cold medicine slumber…"

"Which wasn't an easy thing to do," said PaleoJoe.

"And we charged out after Sadie with the dogs and sleds and just about all the Dolgans along to help," finished Bruno.

"I'm glad Sadie wasn't hurt," said Dakota. "We heard her yelp. We were afraid Dimitri had hurt her."

"That squinty-eyed rabbit man kicked her in the ribs. Nothing broken, only bruised," said Bruno. "Our Sadie is as tough an arctic creature as the Woolly Mammoths!"

Sadie perked up her ears at the mention of her name and gave a happy bark.

"If it wasn't for Sadie, we might not have found you," said PaleoJoe.

"No might about it," rumbled Bruno, reaching under the table to pat the curly black head of the little dog. "You were well on your way to joining the mammoths in their frozen slumber beneath the tundra."

Dakota shuddered and took a big gulp of his hot milk. Out of the corner of his eye he saw Shelly do the same.

"Now," sniffed PaleoJoe, "down to business. We have two items to discuss: the Blue Tusks and," he held up a piece of paper and waved it in the air, "this urgent message I just received from Malachi."

"What's the message?" asked Shelly.

"Let's just say that there's trouble brewing," said PaleoJoe, "and Malachi needs our help."

CHAPTER THIRTY-NINE

The Adventure Continues

"PaleoJoe, don't worry about those tusks," said Bruno. "I can get them out for you before the really bad weather closes in."

Really bad weather?? thought Dakota in disbelief. *Wasn't* this *bad weather? It was certainly cold weather...*

"I'll see that they get safely back to the Balboa," added Bruno. "It's quite a find, you know."

"Thank you, Kincaid," said PaleoJoe. "I know that the tusks are in good hands."

"Aren't we going to stay and help dig them out?" asked Dakota. He couldn't believe that after all the danger they were just going to go home.

"It's going to take several weeks to get those

tusks out of the frozen ground," said Bruno. "It doesn't look like you should wait around that long."

"What do you mean?" asked Shelly. She didn't like the idea of leaving the Blue Tusks either.

"It's Dimitri," said PaleoJoe.

"What about him?" asked Dakota. He exchanged a look with Shelly across the table. They were remembering their desire to pound that particular bad guy for trying to bury them alive in the frozen earth of Siberia.

"He's gone," said PaleoJoe.

"And if he knows what's good for him he won't turn up again," said Shelly.

"Shelly and I think he was working for Buzzsaw's outfit," said Dakota.

"I think you are right," PaleoJoe nodded. "Especially in light of this telegram that I just received from Malachi. We have to talk about this, you two. It's important."

"What does it say?" asked Shelly leaning forward to listen.

"I'll read it," said PaleoJoe unfolding the paper. He cleared his throat, sniffled, and then began to read. "It says: *PaleoJoe, Urgent you and kids meet with Dr. Xu Jie. Breakthrough on B.S. organization possible. Only you can help. Take Trans-Siberian to Beijing. I'll contact you there. Watch out for individual named Dimitri Markovitch. M. Z.*"

"He was right about Dimitri," said Shelly. "We

certainly did need to watch him!"

"B.S. organization could mean Buzzsaw, right?" asked Dakota.

"Yes. I think that's it exactly," agreed PaleoJoe.

"And so we are supposed to go meet with this *shoe-gee* person," said Dakota. "Well, that sounds about right. Where exactly?"

But Shelly's eyes sparkled like firecrackers. "PaleoJoe," she said breathlessly, because she understood something Dakota had missed. Something that would make leaving behind the Blue Tusks for Bruno to take care of not so difficult after all. "Are we going to *China?*"

"Oh yes," said PaleoJoe. "I think we must. Malachi needs our help."

Dakota felt a tingle of excitement, too. *China*— wasn't that where the Great Wall was? And what about the Forbidden City? That was in China too—in Beijing! Dakota had written a report on that for social studies so he knew a little about it, but he never dreamed he might actually see it someday. "What's this Trans-Siberian thingy?" asked Dakota, almost spilling his hot milk in his excitement.

"It's a railway," said PaleoJoe, a faraway look coming into his eyes. "It's one of the longest railways in the world. And we're going to ride it."

"Awesomeness!" said Dakota raising his mug of milk in a toast. "Here's to the next adventure: Trans-Siberia to the Unknown!"

"To the Unknown!" The echo ran around the table as everyone raised their mugs in salute. Shelly smiled at Dakota across the table. Dakota grinned back, feeling a thrill of excitement tingle along his spine. The Dinosaur Detective Club was safely out of danger, and now they had to go to China to try and stop Buzzsaw's gang from further nefarious deeds.

"The Blue Tusks will be waiting at the Balboa for your return," promised Bruno. "I'll get them out of that frozen cave in one piece. Don't worry."

"We'll go get the bad guys then," said Dakota.

"And when we find them," said Shelly, "they'll wish they had behaved themselves much better."

Shelly winked at Dakota and Dakota waggled his eyebrows back.

The adventure wasn't over yet.

Mackinac Island Press

for the love of reading